BLOOD GENESIS: A SHORT STORY

PREQUEL TO THE BLOOD CURSE SERIES

TESSA DAWN

Published by Ghost Pines Publishing, LLC.

Prequel to the Blood Curse Series by Tessa Dawn

First Edition Print Book Published August 15, 2018

10 9 8 7 6 5 4 3 2 1

Copyright © Tessa Dawn, 2014 All rights reserved

ISBN-13: 978-1-718186-91-0

Printed in the United States of America

No part of this publication may be reproduced, stored in, or introduced into a retrieval system, or transmitted in any form, or by any means (electronic, mechanical, photocopying, recording, or otherwise) without the prior written permission of both the copyright owner and the above publisher of this book.

The scanning, uploading, and distribution of this book via the Internet or via any other means without the permission of the publisher is illegal and punishable by law. Please purchase only authorized electronic editions, and do not participate in or encourage electronic piracy of copyrighted materials.

Your support of the author's rights is appreciated.

Author may be contacted at: http://www.tessadawn.com

This is a work of fiction. All characters and events portrayed in this novel are either fictitious or are used fictitiously. Any resemblance to actual persons, living or dead, business establishments, events, or locales is entirely coincidental.

Ghost Pines Publishing, LLC

To all the unsung heroes, whose names will never be known...

ACKNOWLEDGMENTS

Credits
Ghost Pines Publishing, LLC., *Publishing & Design*
GreenHouse Design, Inc., *Cover Art*
Lidia Bircea, *Romanian Translations*
Reba Hilbert, *Editing*

1

800 BC ~ ROMANIA

"One more night," the pitiless royal guard snickered, puffing out his barrel chest in an unnecessary display of power. "Are you ready to die with the sunrise, *female*?" He spoke the last word with derision.

Jessenia closed her eyes and drew in a deep breath for courage, ignoring the annoying smirk on the simpleton's face, shutting out the sound of his obnoxious baritone voice—yet, it echoed still, ricocheting around the barren room like thunder in a violent storm, refusing to be silenced, refusing to give her a moment's peace.

In an act of contrition, she shrank into a submissive posture and shuffled to the back of the chamber on her knees, hoping to avoid inciting the guard's unpredictable wrath or provoking his violent temper. As she pressed her narrow back against the damp, craggy wall and bowed her head even lower, she tried to ignore yet another garish reminder of her circumstances: the piteous sight of Timaos Silivasi, hanging from the ceiling like a prized slab of meat. He was still unconscious from an earlier lashing, and he appeared as nothing more than a freshly slung carcass, hung out to dry…waiting to be butchered.

Timaos wasn't dead.

But perhaps if the gods were merciful, he would pass in his sleep.

It would be a much kinder fate than dying at the hands of Prince Jaegar's men.

As it stood, his broken wrists were anchored to a rusty hook; his bloodied back was beginning to show signs of infection; and the weight of his dangling torso acted like a cruel, cadaverous anchor, spinning its helpless vessel around and around in slow, macabre circles, the hideous display illuminated by the dungeon's torchlight.

Try as she might, Jessenia could not avoid the heart-wrenching visage of her lover, nor could she avoid the guard's still-echoing question: *Was she ready to die?*

At seventeen summers?

In the prime of her life?

And for what crime—being born a female?

No, Jessenia was not ready to die.

She was *not* content to go to her grave with the knowledge that Timaos would die as well, simply because he had loved her, simply because he had refused to hand her over to Jaegar's savage henchmen. She was not ready to accept her fate—or her lover's. And if, in this barren moment, she allowed herself to think about either consequence any further, especially the horrendous manner in which Jaegar's loyalists intended to slay her, she would surely go insane. For what was still to come—*in the morning*—was far too horrific to contemplate, let alone imagine.

Jessenia bit her lip and grasped her head between her hands, rocking back and forth in a soothing, primal motion, desperate to interrupt the momentum of her thoughts. *Stop it, Jessenia,* she admonished herself. *Do not think about it! Just...don't.*

Despite her best intentions, a ghoulish image flashed through her mind: the way she would be forced to kneel at the sacrificial stone like a conquered slave, broken and humbled, before her bloodthirsty conquerors…

I mean it, Jessenia! Stop this at once!

The way Prince Jaegar's soldiers would stretch her slender arms around the stone's wide edges and then bind her wrists to the slab. The intricate cultic knots they would tie—would they actually bite into her flesh?—as they made a barbaric mockery of the original celestial religion…

It doesn't matter. It will be over quickly.

The way the prince's minions would press her head flat against the rock so they could cleanly slice her throat and collect her innocent blood in a once-sacred vessel…

Damnit, Jessenia! Don't do this to yourself!

The way the males would chant and watch—*and cheer*—as her young, innocent blood flowed in crimson rivers, pooling into the urn. The fact that they would grow drunk on the aberrant power of her sacrifice—

Stop this!

Please…

Stop it, now!

All of it was beyond imagining. All of it was beyond comprehension. And she had no doubt, whatsoever, that *all of it* would be beyond her endurance when the time came.

But the time hadn't come.

Not yet.

And thinking about it at this juncture, imagining tomorrow's wicked ceremony, *today*, was an act of utter futility. It wouldn't change a thing. And worse, it would steal away the only thing that mattered: Jessenia's last hours alive with Timaos, the man she loved more than life itself.

She took a deep breath for courage. "The gods will be with me," she whispered beneath her breath. "Surely, they will help me through this, the darkest night of my soul."

The guard roared with wicked laughter, mocking her essential need for solace as well as her very real anguish, as if she were nothing more than a minstrel or a fool to be jeered at. "I wouldn't count on it, sweetheart," he howled.

Jessenia ignored him.

She smoothed out the top layer of her ruffled linen skirts, absently staring at the nearly translucent fabric. Determined to bring her thoughts to heel, she used the garment as a focal object, a mundane point of distraction, something—*anything*—she could concentrate on, in order to escape her looming demise. She got lost in the intricate celestial pattern, so deeply embroidered in the fabric; she drifted away while counting the individual stitches, so neatly gathered along the hem; and she relinquished control while tracing the mystical lines, all in an effort to keep her mind *quiet*, to force her psyche to simply float away, to *just let go* and find sanctuary in the solace of her soul.

As her fingers continued to work absently, tracing the familiar lines and angles of the garment—she had sewn this dress herself, after all—her breathing began to deepen, and she gradually refocused her thoughts.

She would not give the cruel ones her last hours.

She would not yield her mind along with her body.

These final moments belonged to her and Timaos, should he ever awaken.

Just then, the strangest thing happened: It was as if Jessenia's soul took flight, passing through the veil of her garment like a hawk soaring through the mist of a cloud. Although she was a child of astrology, descended from both humans and celestial gods, this was unusual, even for her kind.

The hard earthen floor of the dungeon disappeared, and she found herself soaring at enormous speeds through a hazy blue-gray sky. The very air around her became electrified, as if it were charged with spectral energy, inhabited by unseen ghosts, and the density transformed as well: The clouds were like thick roiling scrolls, ebbing, flowing, and unfolding in mystical layers, right before her eyes. The filmy centers transmuted into opalescent hidden symbols, illuminating the sky like living glyphs that had suddenly come to life. Time became insubstantial, neither here nor there, as the past, present, and future all blended into one seamless tapestry of interwoven knowledge.

Jessenia blinked several times, trying to understand what had just happened, trying to make sense of all that drifted before her, even as she struggled to divine the cryptic but important meaning, the message suspended in the clouds.

The past sped by first—images, impressions, and memories—as she watched, breathed, and became a part of the living history. She watched as the celestial deities descended from the Valley of Spirit and Light and mingled with the human population. She breathed in the story of her race being born. She became the traditions, the magic, and the beauty that defined a new civilization, and she gloried in the gifts her race had been given, in the knowledge, strength, and wisdom they had literally *become*.

And then she sat back, a passive observer, as several centuries passed by, as new generations were born and older ones died off. She watched the rise of the royal family, King Sakarias and Queen Jade; she celebrated the birth of their noble children, Jadon, Jaegar, Ciopori, and Vanya; and she knew—*she intrinsically understood*—what the royal offspring meant to the kingdom.

And then the clouds grew darker, the scrolls grew heavier, and the glyphs became enigmatically dense. She watched as Prince Jaegar grew into manhood and the madness descended upon him. She literally saw the dark, inky roots of demonic suggestions take hold in his mind. She watched his soul turn black, his bloodlust peak, and she shivered with the awareness of what was to come: an insatiable thirst for power amplified by malevolent pride; a ravenous hunger for supremacy, born of the desire to be like the gods; and an army of envious males who would sacrifice their own women—their mothers, sisters, and daughters—in a tainted grasp for control. She could hear the maniacal voices that whispered in their heads, incessantly bidding them to kill…kill…*kill*.

Jessenia watched as the kingdom reacted far too slowly to Jaegar's rise to power, failing to grasp the full breadth of his plan, the full depth of his evil, until it was far too late. She held her breath as, one by one, she observed the males—those who were not yet corrupt, those who had not yet shed blood—coalesce around Prince Jadon in order to form a resistance.

The resistance had been too weak.

Too late.

Too finite.

And then, just like that, the past and the present merged into the future, and Jessenia's eyes grew wide with the wonder—and the horror—and the magic of what unfolded before her:

Blood…

As far as the eye could see.

It consumed the moon, the skies, and the rivers…

Everything was tainted by the *blood of the slain*.

And somehow, in a desperate act of retribution, in an all-consuming haze of madness, the *blood* had its final reckoning: The collective crimson soul of the murdered females rose up like a phoenix from the ashes, clawed its way out of torture and pain, and *cursed* the houses of Jadon and Jaegar, all the while desecrating the original religion and forever altering the future…

Infinitum.

Jessenia shuddered as she beheld the Curse.

As she tried to grasp the twisted reasoning of the females as they doled out the males' punishment:

Sin *for* sin.

Blood *for* blood.

Life *for* life.

The accursed were forced to roam the earth in darkness as creatures of the night.

They were condemned to feed on the blood of the innocent and stripped of their ability to produce female offspring.

They were damned to father twin sons by human hosts who would die wretchedly upon giving birth, and the firstborn of the first set would forever be required as a sacrifice of atonement for their fathers' pagan sins.

And last, but not least, they were banished from their ancient Romanian homeland, never to dwell in the mountains of Transylvania again.

The scope of the Curse was inconceivable.

The repercussions were unimaginable.

And dear goddess of mercy, it was placed upon the sinners' sons —and the offspring of *those* sons—and all the progeny who would be born thereafter, without clemency, without reprieve…without end.

If Jessenia had been standing on solid ground, she would have staggered backward, but as it was, she could only remain in ethereal form, flowing with the vision, gawking and listening as she watched Prince Jadon fall upon his knees and *beg* the Blood for mercy.

As she listened to his haunted plea for grace.

Incredibly, the Blood heard his cry, or at least it found sincerity in his argument, because it offered Prince Jadon—and his line of descendants, alone—four incredible *mercies:*

Although they would still be creatures of the night, they would be allowed to walk in the sun. Although they would still be required to live on blood, they would not be forced to take the lives of the innocent. While they would never produce female children, they would be given one opportunity—*over thirty days* —to obtain a mate, a human *destiny* chosen by the gods. And the woman would be marked by an emblem on her wrist that would match a sign in the heavens.

Although they would still be required to sacrifice a firstborn son, their twins would be born as one child of darkness and one child of light, and they would be allowed to sacrifice the former, while keeping the latter, in order to preserve the celestial race.

What she heard next had no conventional meaning to Jessenia.

There was simply no historic context, no concrete concept in her language, no facet of her imagination she could use to interpret such terms.

Yet and still, the words sent shivers down her spine…

Vampyr.

Nosferatu.

That which lusts for blood.

As distinctly as Jessenia heard the words, as rapidly as she interpreted the vision, another revelation came on its tails, only this one left her breathless with wonder.

At long last, it supplanted her dread with hope.

Jessenia saw a magnificent purple sunset heralded in the clouds. The skyline was dotted with snowcapped mountains. The earth was peppered with radiant blossoms. And there were babbling brooks flowing into crystal-clear rivers; lush green meadows set beneath copper-red canyons; and breathtaking arroyos concealing glorious waterfalls, each one flowing like a pool of liquid diamonds cascading out of a hidden crag. And somewhere in the distance, like a desert mirage, she saw the outline of a man, a once-familiar boy—a ten-year-old child she had seen around her village.

She saw the son of Sebastian and Katalina Mondragon.

And he was all grown up.

He was noble and proud, powerful beyond imagining.

And most of all, *he remembered…*

He recalled the celestial ways. He maintained a divine connection to the stars. He *survived* the bloodlust, the aftermath of the Curse, and he rebuilt the house of Jadon.

Jessenia strained to look closer.

She wanted to burn the image into her mind, to bury it deep within her heart, to protect it like the hidden treasure it was so she could draw on it for strength in the morning.

But it vanished as quickly as it had appeared, giving way to another vision: the faces of five children, a single generation of a band of brothers, all lined up beneath an archaic ceremonial banner, each one reflecting the features, the bearing, and the pride of someone she utterly cherished—Timaos Silivasi.

Her breath whooshed out of her body.

It couldn't be.

Timaos was to be executed in the morning, *right before her*. Did this mean he would somehow survive?

She furrowed her brow and looked closer, searching the children for raven-black hair, scanning for forest-green eyes, examining each set of features for the sharp, handsome angles and the smooth, flawless planes, probing for evidence of her lover's distant lineage. And, one by one, as she studied Timaos's offspring, she thought she heard their names. Like whispers on the wind, the monikers came to her in a mystical song: Marquis, Nathaniel, Kagen, Nachari, and Shelby…

Silivasi.

She stored each name in her memory, entombed each one in her heart, soothed by the knowledge that they were strong, that they were *warriors*, that they were *evidence* of a future.

A future that may or *may not* come to pass…

Jessenia gasped as the final vision became like a lunar portrait, and a far more threatening prophecy was unveiled before her eyes: Ravi Apostu, Prince Jaegar's high priest, was standing over the exceptional child, Napolean Mondragon, in the back of a cobblestone alley. He had the child pinned to the wall with one hand and was about to remove his heart with a rapier. The era was *the present*. The place was Romania. And the time was *tomorrow,* late afternoon.

Just hours before sunset.

Just hours before the *Curse*.

Somehow, the high priest had received a vision of his own, several nights back, and he was positively terrified of the child, determined to end his life. So great was his conviction, his fear of the power the boy would possess in the future, that he had told absolutely no one, yet he would stop at nothing to end the young one's life.

Jessenia shook her head in awe as she made the critical connection. Timaos's role in the future was more than important —*it was absolutely paramount.* He would change the course of history by saving a single child. His ancestors, that lyrical whisper of offspring, would never know that he'd lived. Indeed, if he killed the high priest before the assault, Napolean would never know he had interfered, yet one single act of bravery would salvage the entire race.

She shuddered beneath the awesome breadth of this knowledge.

And then, *just like that*, the clouds became mist.

The mist became a veil.

And the veil became a garment, a timeworn dress with intricate embroidery and familiar linen skirts.

And Jessenia Groza was back in the musty dungeon, shivering on a cold, barren floor. Only, this time, she had something she hadn't possessed before: She had an understanding of the past, knowledge of the future, and a reason to survive one more night. No matter what it took, she had to awaken Timaos. She had to make him understand her vision. She had to force him to change his mind, to do whatever it took to appease his captors…to *live* to save the child.

Though the taste of it would be bitter on his tongue, her lover had to go along with her execution. Although he could not—*he dared not*—shed a single drop of her blood, he had to apologize for opposing Prince Jaegar and convince the heartless prince that he had come to see the light—or the darkness, as the case may be.

Jessenia was the last remaining female of a once-noble race.
Her sacrifice would be the completion.
And then, the Curse would come.
Timaos Silivasi had to survive.

2

Prince Jaegar Demir stormed into his royal bedchamber in a rage, seething from the frustration of the day and cursing the celestial gods, the wizard Fabian, his misguided, self-righteous brother Jadon—hell, anyone he could think of.

Le-a sacrificat pe toate!
He had sacrificed them all!
All but Jessenia Groza.

And that was only because Timaos Silivasi had helped her fake her death, staged a phony funeral and burial, and hidden her in his cellar for the last six months! But Jaegar had her now, and she would certainly die on the morrow, her first-blood consumed by both him and the high priest.

Yet and still, the celestial gods withheld their ultimate favor—infinite, immortal power. They still failed to acknowledge his greatness or to bow down to his genius, to name him as one of the divine.

He spat on the floor, uncaring that the spittle festooned rare, expensive marble.

Sure, the *dark lords*, those shadowed twins of the celestial gods, had rewarded him with ever-increasing power. They had bestowed countless favors on all the kingdom's males, including Prince Jadon's misguided rebels, but what did the celestial deities expect him to do? Hunt down the traitorous wizard Fabian, the renegade fool who had escaped into the Transylvanian Alps with Jaegar's royal sisters, leading both of them to a certain death by the elements, the animals, or starvation? Apologize for Fabian's insolence *as if it were his own*? True, the celestial deities had never actually spoken to Prince Jaegar, so he could only surmise or intuit what the gods truly wanted. Still, the wizard had ultimately denied Jaegar and his loyalists the pleasure—*and the necessity*—of such pure, royal, virginal blood as a final offering, and in doing so he had also denied the gods.

Jaegar kicked a lavishly upholstered chair, sending it careening across the opulent room.

A final offering.

The words still made his blood boil.

Only six months earlier, Jaegar had truly believed—*he had been utterly convinced*—that all the females in the kingdom were gone, *sacrificed*, all save his two royal sisters. After all, their queen mother had just died the previous month from a winter's fever, and Jaegar had insisted that his entire band of loyalists publicly mourn her loss. Although Prince Jadon, in all of his misguided compassion, still swore she had died from a broken heart—she had been devastated by Jaegar's "wicked betrayal"—Jaegar knew he had done right by the monarch. While he may not have respected her gender, he had certainly respected her royal blood.

He snorted at the memory, a cross between a snarl and a laugh. The idea that he had somehow killed his own mother was utterly absurd. He had not betrayed his lineage or his celestial origins— he had only, *ever*, sought to make them complete. He had simply come to understand his inherent birthright, to be worshipped beside the gods, and the fact that females were mere vessels, meant to be purified, utilized, and sacrificed on a male's behalf, was simply the natural order of things. It's not as if he would have actually slit the throat of the woman who gave him life, *murdered the royal queen*—or would he?

He shrugged.

It was of no matter now.

Queen Jade's death, while tragic and untimely, had been fortuitous in the end. Prince Jaegar had never been forced to make such a daring decision.

But he had chosen to offer his pure-blood sisters in what he believed, at the time, would be the definitive sacrifice, and he had been willing to let the chips fall where they may—*his father and his brother could be damned*. But that was before Fabian Antonescu had interfered with his plans, spoiling his masterful climax. Just how the wizard had done it, Jaegar still couldn't comprehend. He should not have been able to move so freely about the castle. Thunderstorm or no, he should not have gone undetected on that fateful night.

He sighed.

The girls were food for the crows now, and he did not have the resources or the inclination to search 155 miles of the southern Carpathians for what little was left of their bodies. However, he did have his sisters to thank for the discovery of Jessenia, for surely now, Jessenia's still-beating heart was all that stood between him, the men, and their ultimate goal of divine elevation, being worshipped beside the gods.

Surely the celestial deities would reward him tomorrow.

Prince Jaegar bit down on his bottom lip and shook his head, causing a thick curtain of raven-black hair to fall forward into his eyes. After Ciopori and Vanya had vanished—after Fabian had unknowingly exiled them to their meaningless deaths—Jaegar had anxiously awaited his *final due*. He had stayed up all night, pacing back and forth in the bitter cold, circling the sacrificial stone along the eastern hillside of the castle's tallest battlements like a hungry wolf. He couldn't count the times he had glanced at the dark, ominous sky or squinted to make out a shooting star, a streaming comet, something—*anything*—that heralded a sign from the gods: acknowledgment that he had been strong enough, brave enough, and determined enough to sacrifice *them all*.

As far as he had known then, there were none left.

Each magical heart, each feminine soul, each precious offering had been surrendered to the gods in an exquisite ritual of death, one by one, given in exchange for absolute power. With his sisters gone, the kingdom had been cleansed.

Surely his reward would be forthcoming…

Yet and still, it hadn't come.

The skies had not changed. The earth had not shifted. The males had remained powerful but unchanged.

Something had remained unfinished.

And that's when Jaegar had ordered a district-wide accounting of the kingdom.

The following morning, he had commanded his generals to exhume the bodies of the slain, to check each record of birth against each record of death. Whether they died by natural causes or unnatural sacrifice, his officers were ordered to account for every female descendant of their race, to enumerate every single entry from the last recorded census. The process had taken nearly six months, but it had inevitably led to a solitary, empty crypt—a grave that should have entombed Jessenia Groza's body. And *that* discovery had led to Timaos Silivasi and the dark, hidden cellar beneath his kitchen pantry where Jessenia was being kept, quietly and comfortably, *still alive and well*, residing beneath the ancestral Silivasi home.

Jaegar clenched his fists in agitation.

To think, he could have sacrificed his precious sisters in vain, believing them to be the very last, the ultimate, when all along, Jessenia had remained…

But now—*at long last*—he truly did have the definitive remaining female, and she was indeed the last living woman of their race, the only girl alive in the kingdom. Following the sunrise sacrifice on the morrow, the long-awaited glory would soon be his. And even as he dealt with Jessenia, he was resigned to deal with his father, the king, once and for all.

Nothing would stand in his way.

Just then, there were three heavy knocks on the solid oak door of his chamber; the handle was wrenched to the side, and the heavy panel swung open with a clatter. No one would have the audacity to approach the prince so boldly, let alone enter his living quarters, save one being of seemingly equal status: his twin brother, Jadon.

Jaegar immediately ascended the stairs beneath his sleeping dais in order to gain a tactical advantage. He spun around to face the door as he took a seat on the soft, overstuffed mattress, waiting to regale his visitor.

Jadon approached far more cautiously than he had entered. "Prince," he said, by way of greeting.

Jaegar smirked and answered in kind. *"Prince."*

Jadon took a slow, deep breath before proceeding, which usually meant he had something important to say and was weighing his words carefully. "How is our father today, Jaegar? How does the *king* fair?" His undue emphasis on the word *king* was as loaded as it was unnecessary. Jaegar knew quite well that Sakarias Demir was still the king of their realm, at least for a few more hours. Nonetheless, *His Majesty* was not a Jaegar-loyalist. He did not support his son's lofty quest, and he would not come around in time. In fact, Jaegar had been all but forced to usurp the king's royal army, making each male to a soldier his own loyal charge, and that meant the king was now expendable. "He eats and breathes and sleeps, brother," Jaegar replied glibly. In other words, *he's still alive...for now.*

Jadon's top lip twitched in an involuntary display of anger, causing Jaegar to stiffen: He did not care to have the same argument again, to quarrel over the future role of the existing king in the new male empire. As it stood, Jaegar did not believe Sakarias Demir had a role to play; whereas, Jadon still hoped for a return to the old ways. He resented the imprisonment of King Sakarias by Prince Jaegar; he resented what he considered nothing less than a traitorous coup, and he would have freed the monarch himself if he'd had the strength or the following to do so. But as it stood, Jadon's house of loyalists could not overthrow Jaegar's army, and Jadon's democratic philosophies—however noble, well argued, and impossible to comprehend—could not hold up against the momentum of Jaegar's movement, the supremacy of his bloodthirsty religion, or the alluring promise of domination over the realm. The males' collective hunger for dominion, their slow rise to personal and mystical power, had swept through the kingdom like a wildfire across a dry prairie. More appropriately, it had covered the land like a tidal wave, rising unchallenged from the depths of a great ocean and covering the shores in one powerful, effortless surge.

Jadon, on the other hand, commanded a deep but placid lake. He made impressive waves here and there, but they remained largely ineffective.

"I fear we are going to come to physical blows over this issue one day," Jadon said, his deep, resonant voice ripe with intention.

Jaegar shot back a look of subtle regard. *So his twin did retain his backbone—that was good to know.* "Aye," he said, "I fear we just might—once the final sacrifice is over." He stood up then, no longer feeling comfortable in such a vulnerable position. He paced back and forth across the dais, eyeing his royal bedchamber whimsically. He swept the back of his fingers along the soft, gold-and-ivory coverlet, admiring the expensive fabric; he used his toe to trace a thin marble vein along the pale, tiled floor, observing it circumspectly; and he glanced upward at the enormous crystal chandelier hanging directly above the bed, as if it were a fascinating new discovery.

The behavior was meant to infuriate and dismiss.

It was Jaegar's way of saying, *your objections and your warnings are as trivial to me as this lavish décor. Yes, I see it—or hear it, as the case may be—but I hardly pay it any mind.*

He then made an elaborate show of sighing, his broad, muscular shoulders rising and falling from the effort, before crossing his arms over his chest. He did not want to engage in hand-to-hand combat with his twin.

Not now.

Not here.

Not without his army.

And not if he didn't have to.

He tried to soften his voice. "We may very well come to *blows* one day, dear brother, but that is not my wish." He met his gaze directly. "*My prince*, I would have never seen such discord grow between us, not when we are—"

Jadon threw up his hand in a curt gesture of dismissal. "Save it for your minions, Jaegar, those who still hang on your every word. I would rather just speak honestly, if you don't mind."

Jaegar's hackles rose. "Do not dare to silence me, brother," he warned. "You would do well to remember where you are and who you are with." He took a deep breath, reaching for a more even temperament. "*You* sought an audience with *me*. *You* are standing in *my* bedchamber. You may very well have objections, but *I* have control over the kingdom's army." He leveled a cautionary gaze at Jadon and held it a couple seconds longer than necessary. "Remember who you're speaking to, brother. And remember who is keeping *our father* alive."

Jadon's dark, placid eyes flashed with unspoken fury, even as he slowly nodded in compliance, squelching his simmering rage. "Forgive me, Prince Jaegar." He somehow managed to speak each word with subtly obscured mockery. "I do get rather *passionate* about these issues." If poison could have materialized as a hidden snake from his tongue, it would have slithered along the floor, glided up the dais, and sank its seeking fangs into

Jaegar's royal throat—such was the venom beneath Jadon's words. But as it stood, Prince Jadon withdrew his challenge and further acquiesced, averting his eyes in feigned respect. "You see, it's just that I've heard it all before." His voice remained steady and congenial as he pressed on. "We are brothers, twins of royal blood—*pure blood*, if you will. And like you, I am a male, and my birthright is to rule at your side, to share in equal dominion over all the creatures that roam our planet, including our own celestial kind." He cocked his eyebrows and squared his jaw. "Am I close?"

Jaegar bit his tongue.

At least the soft-hearted ass had been listening.

He turned on his heel, rounded the majestic bed, and made his way to the ornate nightstand, where he raised a golden goblet, took a deep gulp of wine, and then sat down on the mattress, angling his body to face his sibling. He swept his right hand in a wide arc. "By all means, continue, brother."

Jadon declined his head in a parody of a bow. "Perhaps it is petty of me to speak on behalf of our women"—once again, he mocked Jaegar with his deliberately soft words—"although I should point out that there is only one woman left to speak of at this juncture." He raised his chin and met Jaegar's gaze head-on, his own expression absent of provocation. "As you have so often pointed out, despite the fact that our women are—*were*—the keepers of our magic, the vessels of our secrets, the ones bestowed with our most enchanted, generational knowledge, they are, after all, *only women* and easily exchanged with their human counterparts in our beds. We can still father heirs." He smiled, revealing only a bare hint of teeth. "Such as those *heirs* might be."

Jaegar nodded, even as he plastered a fabricated smile on his own face—Jadon was not the only one who could pretend to be pleasant while smoldering inside, and Jaegar was not about to give his twin the satisfaction of a reaction. Rather, he reclined on the bed, crossed his feet at the ankles, and linked his arms behind his head, sinking deep into the golden brocade pillow. And then he simply waited for his twin to continue.

"And last but not least," Jadon said, ignoring the cheeky display, "it is useless at this point to grieve over the loss of our sisters, or our royal queen mother; after all, princes—*nay, future kings*—were born and bred to carry a heavy yoke, and ours has been heavier than most. But our cause remains—what is the word you like to use?—ah yes, *divine*." He paused, just long enough to draw a needed breath. "And we *will* reap our due harvest in the end." Jadon extended his bow to the waist, as if he were a mere bard completing a performance for the king. "Did I leave anything out, *dear brother*?"

Jaegar's nostrils flared as he sucked in air in a flustered attempt to restrain his temper: Jadon had always possessed the most infuriating manner of wielding his tongue like a sword while keeping it sheathed in its scabbard. He could slice someone open without dampening his smile. He could injure with his tone without modulating his voice. He could cut one to the quick while still remaining agreeable. One way or another, Jadon always made his point.

"Indeed, you have left something out," Jaegar replied, forcing his own voice to remain affable.

Jadon cocked his eyebrows. "And what would that be?"

"Brotherhood," Jaegar said. "Loyalty and comradery."

Despite his superior self-control, Jadon laughed.

"Do not jest," Jaegar snapped. "'Tis not funny in the least." He rose up on the bed, braced the bulk of his weight on his arms, and glared at his brother in challenge. And then he quit pretending—this was no longer a game. "You are my brother, Jadon Demir. Flesh of my flesh. Blood of my blood. We shared our mother's womb for nine long months. And despite this unfathomable weakness, your compassion for all things beneath you—*for all creatures that will never be your equal*—you are still one of the most intelligent, talented, and insightful men I know. You are a better strategist than myself; you are a better tactician than my generals; and you are the only male left in this kingdom who carries pure, royal blood in his veins, save our father, of course. *But his time has passed.*" He curled his lips into a defiant smirk, daring the prince to interrupt. "I would have you by my side, Jadon. And moreover, I would not see our kingdom torn in half, divided by civil war"—he sat fully upright then and leaned forward—"a war you cannot and *will not* win." He narrowed his gaze, and this time, he regarded his brother with esteem, if not outright respect. "And if I know you —*and I believe I do*—you will not stand back and watch as all of your loyalists are slaughtered unnecessarily. You will not send them to their premature deaths by forcing them to wage a battle that has already been lost. *And for what gain?* Jessenia Groza is the last. As you so eloquently put it, soon we will reap the harvest we have planted." His voice grew thick with conviction. "Stand with me, brother. Let us bury our past grievances, even as we bury this last female…*together*. United, we will be the most powerful monarchy that ever lived. Soon we will be as great as the gods."

Jadon took an unwitting step back.

It was almost as if his legs faltered beneath the loathsome weight of Jaegar's words. He shook his head slowly—*sadly*—and then he opened his mouth to speak, promptly closed it, and tried again, this time clearing his throat. *"Jaegar…"*

Jaegar shrugged. "Yes?"

"Brother…"

Jaegar wanted to wring his neck. *"What?"*

Jadon pressed his lips together and furrowed his brow. He clasped his hands behind his back and held the pose for what seemed like an eternity. When, at last, he unlinked his fingers and held both hands up in a gesture of surrender, Jaegar's ears perked up: *Could it be—gods be merciful—was Jadon finally coming around?* He held his breath until he could no longer stand the suspense. *"Well?"*

As if at a momentary loss for words, Jadon continued to shake his head. "If I cannot appeal to whatever is left of your conscience, if I cannot get through to your soul, then perhaps I might appeal to your pride—nay, to your reason—to your extraordinary instinct for self-preservation."

The air left Jaegar's body, and he released it with a snarl. "Do tell, brother."

"You say that soon we will reap the harvest we have planted, and I agree."

Jaegar cocked his eyebrows and waited.

"But not in the way that you think." He gestured insistently with his hands, his voice growing hoarse with conviction. "Jaegar, prince of these Carpathian Mountains, ruler of our beloved homeland; you have complimented my intelligence and my insight, so do me the favor of hearing me now. *Listen to my words.* I swear to you by all that is holy—*brother*—I have a terrible feeling about this sacrifice, an ominous foreboding about the next few days. I am filled with an overwhelming sense of dread."

Jaegar simpered with disgust. *Not this.* Not again. "Of course you are."

"No!" Jadon's fevered voice echoed through the chamber like a bolt of lightning, rattling the chandelier. "Do not dismiss me. I am deathly serious, brother."

Jaegar threw up both hands, but he listened…carefully.

"One by one, our women have died at the hands of their fathers, their brothers, and their sons, slain by those who should have been their protectors. And yet, there has been no reprisal. Piece by piece, the monarchy has been decimated, until you and I are all that remain of a once great kingdom, *us* and our broken, conquered father. Yet and still, the heavens have remained silent. *And now this?*" He pointed in the direction of the eastern battlements, signifying the hill beyond the walls, the sacrificial stone. "Yesterday, you discovered that there is yet one female living, and tomorrow, you would end her life in a sacrifice to the gods—you still seek to perform one final offering, to break the last fragile link in a long chain already stained with blood. But I tell you, brother, the fates will not remain silent forever. So much carnage cannot remain unnoticed. Such sinister crimes cannot remain unanswered, unchallenged—*unavenged*—forever. By all that is still holy—and all that ever was—I implore you: Do not do this thing, Jaegar. Let Jessenia live." He took several steps forward, stopping just shy of the bottom stair on the dais. "She is still young. She may yet have children, perhaps many daughters. And those children may have daughters of their own. Men can father sons well into old age—we may yet reclaim our civilization." He paused to take a labored breath. "And even if we don't, even if she can't, we may yet reclaim our humanity. Jaegar, please listen to reason. There is nothing more to be gained by slaughtering this innocent one—if the gods were going to exalt us, they would have done so already. I fear that what is to come is an abomination, the physical manifestation of a spiritual perversion. Let her live, Jaegar. Restore Father to the throne, and I will bury whatever ill-regard remains between us. I will unite my house with yours in an effort to move the kingdom forward." He shook his head in regret, his deep, contemplative eyes darkening with sorrow. "And if our future generations are to be sired with human women, those not begotten of gods and men, then so be it. At least we will retain our souls. And Jessenia will preserve our legacy."

Jaegar stared at Jadon in stunned stupefaction, silent for what felt like ages. And then he broke out in raucous laughter. "Oh, Jadon. You truly never give up, do you?' He stood up abruptly, watched as his twin took three judicious steps back, and then bounded down the stairs, strolling within inches of his rival. He clasped him by both shoulders. "Brother, you think too much." His voice hardened. "You fear too much. There is nothing on this planet to challenge us, nothing to be afraid of. Don't you get it? *There is nothing greater than us.*" He bent over and placed a familial kiss on Jadon's right cheek. "Tomorrow is a new beginning. You have tonight to decide where you stand. Either way, we will meet back at the castle at dusk, following the execution, where you and I will convene in the great stone hall before the hearth of our ancestors." He relaxed his grip and softened his voice. "We will forge a new covenant then. Whilst our men gather together in the courtyard...*at last*, our kingdom will become unified. All-powerful. *Divine.*" He savored the last word on his tongue. "And as for the future, the direction we will take going forward, you and I will decide this *together,* then." He smiled, feeling suddenly light of heart. "Oh, Jadon, just wait. This time tomorrow we will be as gods—I swear it."

As if Jaegar's hands were burning Jadon's flesh, the prince brushed them off his shoulders and slowly backed away. "Then that's it?" he said, his voice clearly despondent. "There's nothing I can say?"

Jaegar stiffened and met his brother's reproving gaze. "There is one thing." He scowled with disappointment. "You can answer one question...*correctly.*" He leaned forward. "Will you and your loyalists be at the execution tomorrow? Will you take part in this one final sacrifice?"

Jadon nearly recoiled. "No." His voice brooked no argument. "You know that we will not."

Jaegar dropped his head into his hands. He brushed his thick, wavy hair out of his eyes and yanked the ends in frustration. And then he virtually exploded with anger. He punched Jadon in the jaw, rotated his wrist for good measure, and clipped him with his elbow on retreat. When the prince staggered backward, he lunged forward once again and struck him with a crisp, punitive uppercut, right beneath the chin.

Jadon's head snapped back; his teeth visibly rattled, and it sounded like he may have lost a molar. He stumbled to the side, spit out a glob of blood, and braced his jaw in a trembling, angry hand. And then he stepped forward *and smiled*—a wicked, mischievous grin. He dipped his hand beneath his royal cloak and palmed the hilt of his dagger.

Jaegar took a cautious step back. "So it comes to this, dear brother?" He laughed out loud, all the while eyeing the jewel-inlayed shaft of Jadon's blade. "Mm, I see. Well, at least this is the twin I remember." Without hesitation, he brought his hand to his hip, reached into his own leather scabbard, and brandished his private stiletto, stroking the golden tip like a long-lost lover. "Just say the word, *my prince*, and may the best man win."

Jadon stood there like a grain of sand, caught between two halves of a broken hourglass—he couldn't go forward, and he couldn't go back.

"Tick tock; tick tock." Jaegar clucked the sounds with his tongue, wondering what Jadon was thinking: Was he counting his loyal followers, considering the lives of his men? Or was he thinking about their father and the thin little strand, wrapped around Jaegar's finger, that sustained the king's fragile life? Was he calculating the future, evaluating an outcome he was helpless to change, or was he just now realizing he would never leave the castle alive, should he manage to harm the dark prince? Did he even care at this point? "Well, dear brother? I believe we are waiting on you."

Before Jaegar could goad him any further, something ominous and distant passed through Jadon's eyes; he stood up straight and removed his hand from his blade. "I will *not* attend the sacrifice, and neither will my men." He practically growled the words. "But I *will* give you this one last concession: *This day*, I will not carve your heart from your body."

His voice was much too tranquil.

His eyes were much too opaque.

And his manner was far, *far* too self-assured.

Jaegar took another tentative step back, regarding his twin warily. *What the hell was that?* Feeling more than a little uneasy, he tucked his own dagger back into its sheath and cleared his suddenly rusty throat. "Is that right?" He had to find a way to save face. "Then I shall give you one last concession as well: *This day*, I will not hold your insolence against you. I will pardon both you and your vagabonds a day in advance for failing to attend the sacrifice." He held up his hand to silence his brother, lest the prince say something else stupid. "But know this, brother: You—and all of your loyalists—will be back at this castle by nightfall tomorrow for our reconvening, for our celebration. Fail to show up, and I will set the whole of our father's army—*my army*—against you, and I *will* strike down each of your warriors, to the last man, including your beloved king."

Jadon didn't blink.

He didn't move.

And he didn't react.

And there was something so shadowed, so deep and determined in his eyes that it gave Jaegar another moment's pause. Truly, Jadon must have been harboring a secret. He stared at the recalcitrant prince awhile longer, trying to discern what the great mystery was, before he shuddered and looked away.

Jadon Demir was not a weak man, not by a long shot. And he was not a leader to be trifled with—he had simply been outnumbered, outmaneuvered, and utterly caught off guard by the audacity of Jaegar's movement, by the tenacity of Jaegar's men. Still, the noble prince would willingly die for what he believed in; fortunately, he would not recklessly send others to their deaths for the same. He would not needlessly sacrifice the lives of his followers.

Still, with such strong provocation, he should have drawn his dagger.

He should have tried to plunge it in Jaegar's heart, instead of offering him a concession, however insulting and insidious.

Yet something had stayed his hand.

It was as if he had a greater purpose, a hidden reason to live.

Jaegar knew Jadon would comply *eventually,* but it made him more than a little uneasy that he could not intuit *why*—why his brother would back down from a direct provocation to fight, why he would ignore such a blatant insult.

What the hell was he waiting to do?

Jaegar shook his head brusquely from side to side, trying to dislodge the disturbing thoughts. Blood was thicker than water, and Prince Jadon *would* come around.

He had to.

He was Jaegar's *brother*, after all…

And when the time came, the two of them would rule together, side by side, as more than monarchs. They would rule as gods.

In an act of rare valor, he stepped forward, descended to one knee, and reached out to take Jadon's right hand. Never losing eye contact with the prince, he raised his fingers to his lips, kissed the royal crest of his ring, and then rose, once more, to his feet. *"Lasa cei puternici sa mosteneasca pamantul,"* he whispered softly, still commanding his brother's gaze.

Let the mighty inherit the earth.

3

*E*ver since she'd had the strange vision, the guards had been staring at Jessenia like she was an oracle, or worse, some kind of witch. They had no idea what she had seen, and she wasn't about to tell them. They only knew that something preternatural had happened in that cell, that Jessenia had seen or heard —*or come in contact with*—something incredibly powerful, something beyond the ordinary, and as a result, they were keeping a wide berth between themselves and their prisoner.

Jessenia sighed inwardly, grateful for the reprieve. What did the foolish males think? That she could murder them with her eyes, turn their hearts into frogs with a flick of her wrist, or scatter their wits with a chant? Yes, she was a celestial descendant, just as they were, the progeny of gods and men, and as a female, she possessed an especially powerful magic—she housed a wealth of sacred knowledge in her latent genetic memories—but Jessenia had never been formally trained in the mystical arts. She had never been taught how to wield her power or access her celestial memories. She was the only child of a mother who had died while giving birth, making her father her only mentor, and he couldn't teach what he didn't know: The secrets of the race were passed down through the females, never the males, which only made the wholesale slaughter of the women more impossible to believe.

Jessenia sat down on the floor in front of the thick granite slab and stared at Timaos, who was still unconscious. The guards had finally cut him down, perhaps an hour or so ago, and he was resting fitfully on his side, obviously uncomfortable on the stiff, unyielding cot.

She wished she had some medicine, some salve, to treat his wounds. She had used what little knowledge she possessed to try and ease his pain, heal the worst of his injuries, and now, all she could do was watch him and wait, hoping and praying that she would get a chance to tell him what she had seen in her vision… before the morning came.

She ran a gentle hand through his thick, silky black hair. Even matted with sweat and blood, it was beautiful, just like the man lying before her. To this day, she would never understand what it was about her, why Timaos had taken such a fancy to a skinny, auburn-haired girl who was five years his junior, when he could've chosen any woman in the kingdom.

Unlike Jessenia, Timaos was born to a family of means and political power. He was groomed to be a warrior of great standing in the king's guard, and with his tall, impressive bearing, his broad, muscular build, his rustic yet stunning features and charismatic personality, the sky had been his only limit.

Yet and still, Timaos had pursued Jessenia from the first day they met, though she was only thirteen years old at the time. He had shown up on her humble doorstep each morning, rising before dawn to present her with a bushel of wildflowers from the southern hills. He had taken her on long walks through the mountainside, pointing out secret caverns and hidden valleys. He had beat the living stuffing out of Josiah Draghici for calling her a useless wench on the first day of Andromeda's feast, and he had kissed her for the first time when she was fifteen years old, making her knees grow weak beneath her and her heart flutter like it was colonized by a thousand butterflies, each one swirling madly within her chest.

She sighed, remembering his fervent promises: Despite his parents' desire to wed him to a female of standing, a celestial acolyte, in the autumn of his twenty-first year, he had stood his ground, steadfast in his conviction, refusing to accept the unwanted pairing, insisting that he would marry none but Jessenia the moment she came of age.

And oh, how she had come of age...

In a lush, golden meadow, beneath a bright summer's sun, on her sixteenth birthday, Timaos had shown her what true union was. And whether she lived another two hours or a hundred more years, she would never forget the lithe, graceful arc of his back or the powerful cast of his shoulders, the way his muscles had flexed as he'd held her beneath him…or the way he had spoken her name like a prayer. She would never forget how he'd soothed her innocent fears and awakened her dormant passion, all the while striking a perfect balance between dominance and *reverence*, how he'd made love to her body, her mind, and her soul. She would never forget how he had shuddered and groaned, his smooth, melodic voice giving way to a deep, throaty rasp at that pivotal moment.

She would never forget how he had brought her to ecstasy again…and again.

And again.

Timaos had been the first and the last.

After him, there could be no other—there could be no greater love.

Rising from her perch on the floor, she strolled across the room to the single, barred window, built into the cell, and she stared longingly at the sky, making special note of the familiar constellations. After spending so many months in a dark, chilly cellar, she was grateful to see the opalescent moon; she felt honored to stare at the stars; she felt grateful to just be alive.

Despite their horrific predicament, she cherished every second in the presence of her beloved.

Timaos moaned, and she rushed across the chamber to his side, kneeling beside him with yearning. "My love?" she whispered.

He blew out a tortured breath and sank deeper into erratic sleep.

Jessenia fought back the urge to cry. "Please wake up, Timaos. We only have seven hours left, and there is so much I need to tell you." She glanced toward the dimly lit corridor, just outside the dungeon door, to make sure there were no guards within earshot, and then she leaned over and whispered in his ear. "Timaos, if you can hear me, I need you to make me a vow: You must renounce your part in Prince Jadon's rebellion and beg forgiveness for your transgressions, for keeping me hidden away in your cellar these past six months. You *must* find a way to gain your freedom, no matter what it takes, just so long as you don't spill my blood —*never that*. It would be a sin beyond imagining. There's a curse coming, Timaos, and you must live to see it to fruition, no matter the cost. You must find a way to get to the high priest before tomorrow afternoon and slay him. He is going to murder a child, the firstborn son of Sebastian and Katalina Mondragon, but you cannot let this happen. The child is the key to preserving—*nay, to saving*—all that is good and pure and holy in our race. You must find a way to protect him, though he may never know of your sacrifice. And you must also know that I give you permission to love again, to find your *destiny*, and expand your bloodline. Oh, Timaos, if you do this thing, if you kill the high priest, your nobility will live on forever. Your sons will have sons for many generations, and the world will be changed because of you. There will be light again. There will be hope again. There will be a *happily-ever-after* for those who follow behind you." She laid her head on his chest, careful not to come in contact with any of his terrible wounds, mindful of his lingering pain, and she began to recite an entry from her journal, a song she had written in her sixteenth year, one she had never shared with Timaos before now:

"I've seen a million suns go down,
and pearly white moons rise;
with edges smooth, so softly round,
I've loved your moonlit eyes.
Your ivory smile has been my friend,
your voice seduced my ears;
while lying under olive skin,
I've lived one million years.
Within this love,
my life exists.
I need *so much*, your strength…
your kiss."

Having recited the ballad, she linked her fingers in his, praying that he could somehow feel her touch. By all the gods, he had to know that she loved him, that she would always love him. He had to know that no man could have ever been more gentle, kind, or attentive, that no lover could have ever been more skilled or adept.

He had to know that as tragic as her story was, her life had been blessed…

Because of him.

She was stronger for having known his strength, wiser for having known his insight, and more alive for having known his love.

Surely, the gods were lending her their peace in this moment because Jessenia had no idea how she was keeping it all together. She had no idea how she would endure what was yet to come, when the sun made its inaugural trek across the horizon and she was commanded to make that final walk up the eastern hill…to the executioner's stone.

She did not think she could bear it.

But now, in this unparalleled moment, she would have given

all her days on earth just to see Timaos's eyes: open, alert, and regarding her with love.

"Please, Timaos," she whispered once more, "wake up, my love. Let me see your eyes and hear your voice, just one more time."

∼

Throughout the rest of the night, Timaos Silivasi drifted in and out of a restless sleep, at times rising to the surface of consciousness where he thought he heard Jessenia's voice—and she was speaking softly in his ear—at others, sinking deeper into slumber, becoming ever more mired in an endless void of darkness where all was lost but the fitful dreams…

Timaos had bounced back and forth between peaceful dreams and horrific night-terrors for what felt like time without end. In the tranquil dreams, he was making love to Jessenia, and all was right with the world. But in the dreadful nightmares, he was something else—something primitive, wild, and savage—and the world, nay, the very cosmos from which he was begotten, was inexorably upside down.

Now, as he shifted his battered body against what felt like a hard, cold stone, he felt another nightmare coming on, rising from the shadows of his quiescent mind, ascending like a ghost from the tomb of his unconscious.

He felt the *hunger* rising once again.

The dream always started the same way: The sun was shining over a golden field, and Jessenia was sixteen years old again, waiting for Timaos beneath the low-hanging branches of a willow tree, her luminous, steel-blue eyes filled with an adoring mixture of fear, desire, and anticipation. They had planned this meeting—this union—for months, and as he approached the meadow from the east, just as he had told her he would, she spun around to welcome him.

It was then that the dream began to change.

That Timaos began to change.

All at once, the sun grew dark, fading into the backdrop of the pale-blue sky like a servant dismissed by his master, and then the moon crept forward, subtly taking the sun's place, casting eerie, haunting moonbeams across the land like flickers from a torch in a narrow cavern. And, inexplicably, the light shone a deep, crimson red.

Timaos blinked at the change, the rapid, enigmatic shift, not understanding how such a thing was possible. He shuddered and drew his cloak more tightly around his shoulders, feeling a sudden, rising fear for Jessenia.

He began to prowl toward her, to stalk instead of walk, to move with errorless, feline grace, every muscle in his body both awake and alert. The hard, unyielding ground beneath his feet became soft and pliable, as if he and the land were one, as if he had the power to command the very elements. His senses grew unnaturally acute, inconceivably hyper-sensitive—he could smell the spoor of wolves half a mile away; he could see the tiny ants scurrying about the bottoms of the trees; and he could literally taste Jessenia's desire as she waited for him to approach. He growled, deep in his throat, an animalistic sound, reveling in the new intoxicating sensations, luxuriating in the wonder of his dominance and power.

By all the gods, he felt as if he could leap mountains, soar with the birds, pass straight through matter without sidestepping around it. He felt as if he could wrench the willow tree up by its roots without ever breaking a sweat. And he knew—*he absolutely knew*—that he could move faster than the human eye could see. He could leap from his perch across the meadow and be on top of Jessenia before she ever knew what had hit her.

He could tear into her throat and drink to his heart's contentment, and she would be utterly helpless to stop him.

He chuckled deep inside—such a thing was not even necessary. He could command the female's mind if he chose. He could direct her very thoughts. By all that was sacred, he could tell her what to think, what to believe, and what to feel. She was the perfect prey: beautiful, alone, and unsuspecting. And he could make her say or do—*or want*—anything he chose.

The thought brought him up short.

Dearest Ancestors, what was happening to him?

How could he even consider such a thing?

This wasn't just any female. This was Jessenia, *his beloved*.

The beast inside him snarled, as if battling for control. He tuned into the steady, strumming beat of Jessenia's heart, and harmonized it with his own. The twin beats were like music to his ears, a siren's song calling him to love, to taste, and to feast.

No...

No!

This wasn't right. It wasn't right at all.

What was happening?

Just then, Jessenia raised her graceful hand and waved at him, her brilliant smile illuminating her delicate features, adorning her lovely face...

And he pounced.

He leapt across the meadow in one smooth bound, released his throbbing fangs, and sank them deep into her jugular, tearing through the flesh like a starved, raging beast.

4

SUNRISE

*E*verything happened at once.

Timaos came awake with a shout, shooting straight up on the stone as if trying to flee a horrific nightmare, and three of Jaegar's guards rushed into the dungeon chamber, each dressed in ceremonial garb: one, to take hold of Jessenia; another, to seize Timaos; and the last, to stand in the doorway and watch, lest one of the prisoners try to make an escape.

The first rays of sunlight were peeking over the horizon, shining through the tiny, banded window, and casting ominous shadows against the earthen floor in the shape of three iron bars.

Jessenia knew her time had come.

But it was too soon, much too soon. Timaos had remained unconscious all night, writhing on the stone in response to pain and fitful dreams, and she had not been able to awaken him. Now, as he gasped for air, his deep forest-green eyes wide with the horror of whatever he had seen in his nightmare, her heart raced rapidly in her chest. She had to get through to him, and she hadn't much time.

Spinning around to face him, even as a tall, burly guard manacled her wrists behind her back, she put all the force she could muster into her voice. "You bastard!" she shouted, demanding his full attention. His startled, confused gazed met hers. "You said that you loved me! You said that you would die for me—nay, that you were willing to die *with me*—and yet, all through the night as you dreamed, leaving me here in this cell all alone, you spoke of nothing more than Prince Jaegar's brilliance, of your desire to side with his loyalists." She leveled a hate-filled glare at him, trying to make him understand. "I will never forgive you, Timaos Silivasi. I will haunt you from the grave."

Timaos recoiled on the stone, and in his horror, he bounded to his feet in order to take a step toward her, forgetting the awful wounds on his back. At the same time, the guard who had seized him slammed a fist into his back, and he cringed in inner and outer agony. *"Jessenia..."*

She shook her head in defiance, ignoring his obvious pain. "No, do not speak my name." And then she glanced over her shoulder at the vile brute with a horribly scarred face who was holding her by her bound wrists. "Let me say a final good-bye to this traitor. Give me at least this one last pleasure."

The hideous male glanced back and forth between Timaos and Jessenia, immediately suspicious and wary, and in that one tentative second, he relaxed his hold and she rushed across the room at Timaos. "Hear me now, *warrior*," she spat with disdain, hoping to convince the guards to let this play out. She immediately switched her tongue to Latin, praying that the sentries were too uneducated to understand her words. With his privileged upbringing, Timaos had been schooled in all the principal languages, and he had taken it upon himself to teach several of them to Jessenia, Latin being the first.

"Listen to me, my love," she began. Although her words were desperate and caring, she was careful to keep her voice harsh and accusing. She wanted the guards to think she hated him. "We only have moments, and you *must* hear my words. I do not have time to ask you about your nightmare. I do not have time to say my goodbyes, but what I tell you now is of the utmost importance. If you ever loved me, then hear my words."

Timaos blinked several times in quick succession, almost as if he were still trying to pull himself out of the nightmare, as if he were struggling to process such rapidly changing events. Yet and still, to his credit, he held his tongue and locked his gaze with hers, listening intently.

"I love you eternally, Timaos, and I always will. But you must renounce your rebellion. You must convince Prince Jaegar that you were wrong to oppose him, wrong to hide me in the cellar all this time. You must do whatever it takes to live!"

Timaos shrank back in disgust, and in his confusion, he forgot to speak in Latin. "Jessenia, *no*…do not do this. I will never, *ever*—"

She raised her voice and shouted over him, as if they were having a heated argument. "Timaos, shut up and listen!" He blanched, and she took a deep breath, forcing herself to continue. "I saw a vision of the future, and I know that it is true. If you ever loved me, if you ever trusted me, then hear me now: Before the sun sets this night, *every* male in this kingdom will be punished—they will be changed into vile creatures of the night, forced to feed on the blood of the innocent. They will be *cursed* by the blood of the slain, but Prince Jadon will beg the apparition for mercy." She knew it sounded insane, beyond fantastical, *impossible*, but she had to make him understand. She had to make him believe her. "Do not question me, Timaos. It *will* come to pass. And you—you have a critical role to play in the future. All that our race has ever been —or ever will become—is dependent upon the survival of a single child, and his life is in great jeopardy. You must survive to protect him, to slay his enemy before the Curse comes to pass. You must destroy the high priest, Ravi, before mid-afternoon today." She gasped for air, trying desperately to organize her thoughts and speak her entire piece before their time was cut short. "You will be the father of many generations, and your descendants will be strong, proud, and honorable. They will be good men, as the gods always intended. Stay alive, Timaos! No matter what it takes, *you must stay alive*. You must pretend to side with Prince Jaegar and then pledge your formal allegiance, once again, to Prince Jadon before the Curse occurs."

The disfigured guard who had inadvertently released her was quickly losing his patience. He stepped forward, grabbed her by her shackled wrists, and wrenched her backward, tugging her away from Timaos and dragging her to the door of the cell. Timaos started to lunge toward him, no longer restrained by his baffled guard, and she shook her head furiously, begging him with her eyes to play along.

"Siste!" *No!* she shouted in Latin. "Please, pretend to hate me, Timaos. Do not fight this useless battle. Fight for the only thing which matters, the only thing our race has left—*the future*." As she struggled to keep her balance and slowly backed away, she gazed into his eyes one last time, wishing she could stay there for all eternity. "Timaos, please, *promise me*."

He gasped, but he stopped rushing toward her. He halted his suicidal lunge at her guard, and his throat worked convulsively as he fought to swallow his anger and frustration. The muscles in his arms literally twitched with the need to strike out, to fight for his beloved one last time, but *bless him for his courage*, he restrained the impulse.

He just stood there staring into her eyes…and shaking.

Holding his tortured gaze, she nearly faltered, but she drew a deep, steadying breath, stiffened her spine, and bit down on her torment. "Remember, once I am gone, you must seek out the high priest and destroy him. *Kill him, Timaos*, no matter what it takes! And then pledge your loyalty anew to Prince Jadon—if you do not, you will not receive the Blood's mercy."

The pained look of betrayal that swept over Timaos's face was agonizing in its intensity, and the breath rushed out of Jessenia's body. He was beyond horrified. He was beyond dazed. He was the walking, breathing embodiment of grief. It was evident that he did not want to live without her. He would rather die fighting than live by paying homage to her enemies. She knew him all too well.

"*Jessenia...*" He breathed the word like a prayer, his haunted voice trailing off on a rasp. His eyes and the slight shake of his head said all he couldn't say: *I love you. Please forgive me if I don't comply.*

Jessenia wilted, feeling as if the battle had already been lost, as if her life *and their love* would ultimately be lost, in vain. This time, she allowed true tenderness to reach her eyes as she nodded. "I know," she whispered, "*ego quoque te amo.*" *I love you, too.* Then still speaking in Latin, she added, "But if you love me, *because you love me*, do this one last thing for me. Let me go, Timaos. There is no help for me. There is nothing to be gained by your death. But if you live to bring about a brighter future, so that my death—so that *all* the senseless deaths—will not be in vain, then all that we had will live on." As the impatient guard dragged her out of the doorway, she tried to study each one of Timaos's features one last time. "Remember, *always and forever*, that I loved you more than all the stars in the celestial skies, that I always have, and I always will."

Timaos staggered where he stood.

His powerful, masculine knees buckled beneath him, and he sank to the floor in a heap of affliction, dropping his head in his hands.

He couldn't reply.

His only answer was a plaintive moan.

Jessenia could not bear to watch him suffer. She could not bear to prolong this wretched good-bye. Gathering her courage, she turned away and let her captor lead her down the inner corridor of the ancient dungeon, toward the final holding cell where they would prepare her body for sacrifice. After that, they would take her outside, usher her through the Courtyard of Justice, and then lead her up the steep, grassy slope to the executioner's stone, where they would offer her blood to the gods.

She fought to keep from trembling as she mindlessly placed one foot in front of the other and tried to walk a straight line, and then she felt the ground quake beneath her, the earth shift back and forth on its plates, and she instinctively knew it was a metaphysical phenomenon: The earth itself was reacting to Timaos's grief.

She could only hope that he had heard her, that he would heed her dying wish.

That he would do whatever it took *to stay alive* and destroy the wicked priest.

～

Timaos Silivasi stared blankly at the floor, his mouth hanging open, his mind spinning in dizzying circles, in nauseating waves of disbelief.

What the hell had just happened?

And what the hell was he supposed to do?

Every cell in his body wanted to rise up and rebel, to use all his years of martial training to fight—to lash out and kill as many of Jaegar's guards as he could before they struck him down.

Before they dragged him, much like Jessenia, down the narrow dungeon corridor, outside into the Courtyard of Justice, and finally ended his life.

Took his head on the guillotine.

But he was so deeply confused and conflicted.

He would rather rip out his own innards and consume them as he died than swear allegiance to Jaegar Demir, than pretend to go along with this wicked, soulless scheme. He would rather spend eternity in the Valley of Death and Shadows than a lifetime in the Valley of Spirit and Light if it meant betraying his love for Jessenia.

Just the same, he hesitated.

Jessenia had said so many irrational, unbelievable, unknowable things: The Blood would curse the males? They would survive to create a new civilization, and he would be the father of many generations?

Nay, he would never, *ever* love again.

By all that was holy, he would die of a broken heart the moment Jessenia was gone—she was all he had ever lived for, and the boy child, the one he must save? Who was she speaking of? She had only given him one directive: Kill the high priest before mid-afternoon today. What if he failed? What if he had to make a second attempt? Was there any leeway in her instructions?

He knew so little.

And how the hell was he supposed to get anywhere near Ravi Apostu, alone?

He shook his head in disgust and bewilderment.

None of it made any sense.

Yet Jessenia had been so insistent.

So sure.

He absently pinched the bridge of his nose and tried to focus his thoughts. There was one thing she had said that stuck with him, that almost made sense, like a portent from his nightmare. "Before the sun sets this night, every male in this kingdom will be punished—they will be changed into vile creatures of the night, forced to feed on the blood of the innocent."

It was exactly what he had seen in his dream.

What he had *been* in his dream.

Timaos stared at the desolate floor, ignoring the angry guard behind him who was now cursing in his ear, demanding that he rise.

He had no idea what to do.

Every bone in his body rebelled. If he fought his captors, if he died now, going to his grave like a warrior, he could at least perish in peace, meet his death with his conscience intact. He would see

Jessenia soon after—they would be reunited in the Valley of Spirit and Light—and hopefully, they would live there forever, loving on the other side.

His soul ached with the desire to end it, and still he wondered: *Will she ever forgive me for not heeding her words?* Surely she would understand that he just couldn't do it, that he just couldn't betray all that they were.

He was just about to rise up and snatch the bad-mannered, overblown idiot behind him by the throat when he felt a shattering blow to the back of his head. The guard had struck him with the hilt of his sword…or maybe it was a rock or a piece of…

All the world went black.

5

*J*essenia donned the white virginal gown that her captor gave her without resistance. She braided her hair in extravagant plaits, just as her guard instructed, and then she drank the bitter tea he handed her without hesitating—it was some revolting concoction of herbs meant to keep her from struggling, as if such a thing were possible.

As if it would make any difference.

She tossed the tin cup to the floor with cold contempt.

Nothing mattered at this point—absolutely nothing.

Except Timaos.

Her fate was sealed—she could never fight Prince Jaegar's men. All that mattered was making sure, knowing in the end, that her death had not been in vain.

She could only hope as they led her through the Courtyard of Justice—the ancient ceremonial grounds where accused criminals were brought to trial, where they were tortured into making confessions and then executed on sight—that she didn't see any *evidence* of recent bloodshed. She could only pray that as they led her beyond the ghoulish rack, the wooden stockade, and the chilling guillotine, she did not see any fresh crimson stains. For that would mean Timaos was already dead.

If she could just get through the courtyard unscathed, knowing Timaos survived, then she could somehow endure the rest: the steep walk up the grassy slope to the top of Executioner Hill and then one final trek to the sacrificial stone.

She could get through it.

She had to.

She would be brave if it was the last thing she ever did.

She cringed at the words—of course, it *would be* the last thing she ever did.

She shook her head to dismiss the thought and held her breath, reaching deep within for courage, and then she turned to face her calloused accuser. "I'm ready," she whispered, her voice quaking with the truth of her fear.

The cruel, heartless overseer reached out to thumb her hair, admiring the plaits as if such a thing mattered at all, and then he cocked his head to the side and grinned, exposing a dark, unsightly gap in his teeth. "You are a pretty one," he said crudely. "It's too bad we never spent some *private* time together before today." He shrugged. "But Prince Jaegar is dead set against it, so…*oh well*." His deep, boorish voice trailed off, and Jessenia retched in her mouth, her stomach turning over in disgust.

"Don't touch me," she snarled, spitting the bile out on the floor. And then she added, "Well, at least the black-hearted pig got one thing right in his useless, despicable life."

The guard struck her so fast she never saw it coming, the back of his hand stinging the side of her cheek.

The blow bit into her flesh.

The force stunned her senses.

And the vibration rattled her wits, causing her to stumble back, stagger sideways, and clutch at the stony wall in order to regain her balance. Once she had regained her bearings, she straightened her spine and glared at the degenerate with contempt. *"Go to Hades, you ugly swine!"*

He raised his hand and held it just inches above her uninjured cheek, suspended in an unspoken threat, as he glared at her with hate-filled eyes.

She refused to flinch.

Finally, he lowered it back to his side. "Watch your tongue, wench," he growled, forcing himself to take a levelheaded step back.

Jessenia bit her tongue and averted her eyes. Apparently Prince Jaegar also frowned on beating the sacrifices before their executions, or this brute would have already done it. Just the same, she needed to maintain her composure just a little while longer.

This was not her battle.

Not here.

Not now.

She wasn't about to challenge this caveman any further; but she had to admit, for the first time since she had seen the vision of the Curse, she reveled in the clandestine knowledge: *By night's end, you will be nothing more than a piteous animal, crawling about the ground in agony, wracked with pain and hunger. The torture you visit upon me will be revisited upon you a million fold, for as many years, and I hope you burn in the sun, slowly, like the dark, soulless creature you are.* She spat the words in her mind, and then she reeled at the intensity of their venom.

No, she did not mean it, not a single word.

For the very same torture would be visited upon Timaos if he chose to live, if he fought to survive. It would be visited upon all the followers of Prince Jadon as well.

She swallowed her anger, her fear, and her pride, and she forced herself to press on. "Let's just get this over with," she murmured, stunned at her bravery.

Or stupidity.

The male regarded her from head to toe, as if taking her full measure for the very first time, and he nodded. "Very well," he grunted, pointing toward the dark, vacant corridor, in the direction of the final vestibule to the courtyard. "Walk."

Jessenia took a tentative step forward, realizing she was trembling. She stopped, took a slow, deep breath, and then proceeded to walk more slowly. The ground felt uneven beneath her feet; the cool, damp musk of the corridor smelled especially pungent, and the large wooden door at the end of the hall—thick from its weighty construction, tragic with the silent stories of so many women—loomed like a predator masked in a fog, just waiting to collect its prey. And then the torchlight went out, the guard fumbled with his heavy keys, and the iron lock was opened at last.

Jessenia took three courageous steps forward, stepped out into the Courtyard of Justice, and collapsed.

"Noooooooo!"

Her scream echoed through the square, ricocheted off the hillside, and traveled toward the heavens, wracking her body with grief. Any courage she had possessed, any strength or determination, was utterly and indelibly gone.

The guillotine was stained with fresh crimson blood.

The blade was resting at the bottom of the structure, rather than perched along the top, and on the ground, just beneath the pewter bucket, was a stagnant pool of blood, the hideous stains still oozing along the sides of the bucket.

She wrenched at the fabric of her garment, her uneven nails ripping the cloth. *"Timaos..."* She cradled her stomach with her arms and rocked back and forth in regret. "No, no, no...*no*."

Her captor, who had remained indifferent until then, snatched her by the crook of her arm, yanked her onto her feet, and began to drag her mercilessly behind him, through the Courtyard of Justice, toward the bottom of the hill, and then slowly up the steep, grassy incline in the direction of the inevitable stone.

She kicked and screamed and bucked against him, no longer

caring if she provoked his wrath, no longer caring if she lived or died at this very moment.

All of her courage was gone.

All of her dignity was wasted.

There was only pain and loss and unmeasurable sorrow.

None of this had meant a thing.

Timaos was dead, and she was going to be slaughtered like an animal—Prince Jaegar would win in the end.

Oh dear celestial gods, why?

Why had the great ones abandoned her?

Why had they abandoned her people?

6
---

*T*ime stood still, the heavens grew quiet, and the earth failed to spin on its axis as Jessenia floated in a haze of unreality, as the guard dragged her across the field, along the leafy hilltop, and to the base of the executioner's stone.

The sun seemed unusually harsh, unbearably hot, as the merciless rays shone down upon her in an utter act of hypocrisy: There was no light left in the world. There was no warmth or goodness. The sky could not be blue, and the day could not be peaceful. There was only pain and sacrifice and torture and death.

There was only evil and the triumph of the wicked.

She thought she felt a rough pair of hands pressing against her shoulders, forcing her to kneel, but she couldn't be sure. Her body was numb and her heart was racing, yet her mind was retreating into a cavern of denial, curiously detached from it all.

To the right of her, towering above her, she saw a silhouette of the high priest. He was adorned in all his ceremonial regalia; his dark-brown hair whipped about his collar as if stirred by a turbulent wind, and his cruel, impassive shoulders were hunched forward in an angry, concave line, as if he were the one being affronted. And then Prince Jaegar approached the stone from the opposite side, stooping down to take her full measure —*smiling in the sunlight*—as he spoke her name out loud, before reciting some blasphemous invocation from what was once a sacred religion.

He was a terrifying sight to behold.

His unjustly handsome features were nearly demonic with perversion; his thick crown of hair was like a dark, menacing cloud; and his overbearing presence descended upon her, swirled all around her, like a violent midday storm.

But thank the gods, Jessenia couldn't see his wicked eyes.

She was too far gone.

Too lost in terror, too consumed by grief, to bring him fully into focus.

She was too devastated by the loss of Timaos to think of anything but his plight.

And somewhere in the distance, she thought she heard a recurrent siren, a repetitive, ear-piercing wail, and then all at once it registered—the sound wasn't coming from a distance at all—it was coming from her throat. That gnawing, guttural, inhuman cry was her own piteous protest, her own plaintive moans.

Still, she remained detached.

Lost.

Spinning in a whirlwind of despondency and grief.

And then the priest handed the sacred goblet to Prince Jaegar, the vessel he would use to catch the first drops of Jessenia's blood, *to drink them like a cannibal.* He unchained her hands from behind her back and bound them, once again, about the circumference of the stone. He withdrew an emerald-tipped dagger from the scabbard at his side and stepped silently toward her, even as another pair of hands—*whose were they? She couldn't tell!*—pressed her head to the slab and told her to be still.

Be still?

Be still!

She arched her back and tried to wrench her head free from

the stone, twisting wildly in her desperation, bucking like a wild steed, driven by all-consuming terror.

Oh, gods; oh, gods; oh gods...nooooooo! "Help me!"

The cry crackled through the meadow like thunder, even as the surrounding males began to chant, and then she began to hyperventilate. "No, no, *no*!" She couldn't catch her breath. "Please, please, *please*." The air was much too shallow. "Don't, don't....*don't*!" She was truly lost in a panic.

She was *this close* to losing her sanity.

The priest crouched down to place the blade against her throat, and she utterly lost her way. "Oh, gods, no, no, *no*...please, please, *please*...no, please, no, please, no!" Her body shook like she had tremors and her breath caught in her throat; yet and still, she begged and pleaded and wailed. She couldn't stop. She couldn't help it. She knew her eyes were as wide as saucers. She knew she was only making things worse. If anything, she would only prolong the pain and suffering, but she was entirely out of control.

Prince Jaegar pressed his large, ring-clad hand against the small of her back in an effort to hold her still, and she was struck with a sudden wave of nausea.

Just then, out of the corner of her eye, she saw a pair of freshly pressed trousers drawing nearer to the base of the stone, the elaborate, plaited hems brushing along the ground. The male was adorned in the traditional white-and-red garb of the sacrifice, and as he came closer, she noticed that he also wore the customary band of the house of Jaegar wreathed about his upper right arm. "Jessenia."

He only spoke one word, and her heart stopped racing.

Her body quit protesting, and her mind quit reeling.

Dearest goddess of mercy, it was Timaos.

The blood had not been his.

He bent down to meet her eyes, and his gentle hand took the place of Prince Jaegar's. "Shh," he said, his voice as calm, calculated, and contrived as it was familiar. "This is almost over, female," he said, careful to play his expected role. "Quit fighting it." On one hand, he sounded every bit like a follower of Jaegar—cold, indifferent, and piteously unashamed. But on the other hand, he sounded like the Timaos she knew—artful, determined, and fastidiously in control. "Stop resisting, and it will soon be over."

She parted her lips and measured her breaths. "Timaos?" She knew it was him, but she just had to be sure.

"Shh," he repeated, deepening the pressure of his hand, moving his fingers in small, imperceptible circles, in an effort to lend her his strength. "Just breathe."

He could not say he loved her.

He could not offer her words of comfort or free her from the stone.

As it stood, he was taking a huge risk by approaching her like this, yet he was walking a delicate line with both courage and grace. In a calculated moment of defiance, he glanced askance at the high priest and narrowed his gaze—his pupils were positively glacier—and then he turned his attention back to Jessenia. "Forgive my betrayal, but I have seen a brighter future, and I *know* what I must do."

Somewhere in the background, Prince Jaegar cleared his throat—he may have even chuckled—but Jessenia didn't care.

She understood Timaos's words clearly.

Intimately.

Timaos Silivasi had not betrayed Jessenia. He had not betrayed their love. Rather, he had chosen to betray his own conscience. He had chosen to betray his deep-seated hatred of Prince Jaegar. He had chosen to betray his own will.

Timaos had swallowed his pride, embraced his grief, and chosen to join the lost males in order to comply with her wishes.

Timaos had chosen to live.

He had resolved to kill the high priest, and he had done it for

Jessenia, so her death would not be in vain. He had done it for their people, so that all would not be lost.

He removed his hand from her back, held her gaze one second too long, and then he stood up with iron determination and backed away from the stone. Drawing a deep, singular breath, he began the sacrificial chant once more, and all the males chimed in.

The sound should have terrified her.

The rise and fall of their collective, deep voices, resonating with so much hatred and inequity, should have tormented her soul; but instead, it gave her peace beyond imagining.

It was, indeed, almost over.

Timaos was there—*he was with her*—and she would die with her beloved at her side, in the only way he could be.

She would pass into the spirit world knowing that their love would live on in his heart, knowing that the faces she had seen in her vision, that remarkable generation of males, so noble, proud, and *worthy*, would one day come to pass.

She closed her eyes and stopped struggling.

She stilled her mind and ceased trembling.

She dropped her ear to the stone and relaxed her shoulders.

And then, she began to chant beneath her breath, along with the other males, only the verse she repeated was a very different refrain: *Timaos…Timaos…Timaos.*

～

Timaos Silivasi watched as Jessenia grew enigmatically calm.

As she ceased resisting, stopped begging, and prepared to embrace her passing with both resolution and pride.

With every ounce of his being he wanted to go down fighting, to spare her from this indignity, to defend her life and her body, and to take as many of her executioners to the grave with him as he could. But he would not dishonor her so, not when she had pleaded so valiantly for his submission, not when he had already debased himself in order to convince Prince Jaegar that he'd had a change of heart.

Not when so many future generations were riding on his decision.

Stepping away from the stone, he began the unholy chant, forcing himself to speak the irreverent words with false but convincing conviction.

And then he shut his eyes.

He could not watch.

He *would not* watch.

As the priest brandished the blade once more and ended her precious life.

Rather, he held onto her spectacular vision, he got lost within her dream, and all the while, he replayed her words like a prayer for absolution: *Stay alive. Pledge your allegiance to Prince Jadon. Slay the wicked priest.*

Protect the unknown child with your soul.

He is the key to the future.

Right then and there, Timaos Silivasi made the most sacred pledge of his life: He vowed to do all Jessenia had asked of him, and he swore he would not fail, no matter what occurred.

I will survive this night, Jessenia. I will *survive this curse. By all the gods, I make you this promise: I will pledge my loyalty anew to Prince Jadon, long before it's too late. I will somehow get to the priest, and I will end his miserable life. I will save the boy-child, and I will raise my own sons to be men among men, to cherish the gift of women.*

There will *be a new day, and it will dawn beneath a sky of reverence, hope, and love.*

The legacy of our celestial race will live on.

EPILOGUE

Prince Jaegar Demir reclined on the grassy hillside and gazed out at the valley, just beyond the executioner's stone. He surveyed his vast, prolific kingdom, admiring all that lay before him, and smiled. While King Sakarias's death had been such an unpleasant business—guillotines were such nasty contraptions—he had no regrets. He had followed his conscience and obeyed his religion. He had done what needed to be done.

He sighed with satisfaction.

He had sacrificed them all.

And soon, he would be as a god among men, no longer a celestial descendant, the progeny of gods and humans, but a bona fide lord in his own right, on equal footing with the divine.

And Jadon, he would come around in time.

He had to.

It was his birthright as well as his sacred duty.

Besides, he was Jaegar's brother, and blood *was* thicker than water.

He closed his eyes and listened to the wind sweeping through the trees, reveling in the accompanying sound of celestial voices, the relentless summoning of the gods, as they called to him, almost incessantly now: *"Come to the castle, Prince Jaegar. Come to the royal hall. Bring your brother, Jadon, and both of your loyal houses. Come and receive your due."*

Jaegar shivered with anticipation.

It would not be long now.

∼

The Blood of the slain *congealed*.

It bonded together, rose in an arc, and roiled with barely concealed fury, pacing wildly through the royal hall of the now-haunted castle, waiting to make its pronouncement, waiting to wield its Curse.

Vengeance would be swift in coming and oh so very sweet when it came.

Jessenia Groza had been the last female of their race to die, the only woman left in the kingdom, and now she, too, rested with the ancients.

Such blasphemy would not go unpunished.

Such heresy would not be allowed to stand.

The Blood hissed and fumed and smoldered as hatred warred with vengeance for supremacy, and all-consuming rage took root, planting its feral claws on the cold stone floor.

Waiting.

Anticipating.

Salivating…

Ah yes, he was so arrogant, so sure of himself, so ripe for the picking with his bloodstained hands.

It would not be long now.

"Come to the castle, Prince Jaegar. Come to the royal hall. Bring your brother, Jadon, and both of your loyal houses. *Come and receive your due.*"

A NOTE FROM THE AUTHOR

Dear Readers,

While the prequel to the Blood Curse Series takes place in ancient times, the series itself is set in the modern world, in a Rocky Mountain valley called Dark Moon Vale. It begins with the individual stories of the Silivasi brothers (the descendants of Timaos) and the story of their ensuing Blood Moons as each male discovers his long-awaited *destiny*...and the chance to love that eluded Jessenia and Timaos.

In addition, it answers many lingering questions along the way: What happened *inside and outside* of that castle on that fateful day? Whatever became of Napolean Mondragon, that important ten-year-old child? And why did Prince Jadon hesitate when confronted by his evil nemesis, his brother Jaegar?

The ongoing battle between good and evil—the house of Jadon and the house of Jaegar—remains the backdrop as the Curse and the thirty-day Blood Moon play out again and again...

Only this time, the noble warriors strike back.

BOOKS IN THE BLOOD CURSE SERIES

Blood Genesis (prequel)
Blood Destiny
Blood Awakening
Blood Possession
Blood Shadows
Blood Redemption
Blood Father
Blood Vengeance
Blood Ecstasy
Blood Betrayal
Christmas In Dark Moon Vale
Blood Web
Blood Echo ~ Coming Soon

ALSO BY TESSA DAWN

DRAGONS REALM SAGA

Dragons Realm

Dragons Reign

PANTHEON OF DRAGONS

Zanaikeyros ~ Son of Dragons

Axeviathon ~ Son of Dragons (Coming Soon)

NIGHTWALKER SERIES

Daywalker ~ The Beginning

(A New Adult Short Story)

JOIN THE AUTHOR'S MAILING LIST

If you would like to receive a direct email notification each time
Tessa releases a new book,
please join the author's mailing list at

www.tessadawn.com

A SNEAK PEEK FROM BLOOD DESTINY

(BOOK #1 – BLOOD CURSE SERIES)

The dark woods were eerily quiet. Not a single sound invaded the night. Not even the soft hooting of an owl overhead or the faint rustle of leaves in the trees as an icy wind swept through the darkness. The ancient, circular clearing was on hallowed ground. A spherical graveyard surrounded by tall, looming pines and enormous, jutting rocks—the final resting place for the fallen descendants of Jadon.

Nathaniel Silivasi knelt before a perfect, lifeless body as it lay unnaturally still upon an ancient stone slab. His fraternal twin, Kagen, crouched down beside him.

His heart was heavy with sorrow—his grief overwhelming. The gravity of the loss was almost too much to bear.

It was still hard to believe that their youngest brother had fallen. *Shelby:* the last born of the five, a soul so full of mischief and humor. *Shelby:* vibrant, powerful, and gifted beyond measure.

Only five hundred years old, he had died as a mere fledgling. Just another proud warrior lost to the original sin.

Nathaniel cursed the heavens against the fate of their kind.

Like all descendants of Jadon, he was a being of both darkness and light, a powerful prince of the night, protecting the earth and its inhabitants from the darker demons of their species—the descendants of Jaegar.

He bowed his head in silent resignation, trying to accept what could never be changed: Shelby had failed to complete his destiny, to obtain the one human woman tied to his infinite soul, the only being in a lifetime of immortality who could free him from the ultimate claim of the Blood Curse.

With piercing eyes the color of emeralds and long black hair that flowed like the wind, Dalia Montano's path had been chosen long before her birth. Chosen for Shelby and the future of their race.

It had been Dalia's fate to bear Shelby's twin sons: a child of light, who would forever lift the dark curse of death and spare his soul from eternal damnation, and a child of darkness, who would be offered in atonement for the sins of their forefathers.

Nathaniel trembled as the memory replayed in his mind.

Shelby had immediately recognized all the signs—just as he should have—the bloodred moon, the sudden appearance of his birth constellation in a pitch-black sky, even the matching birthmark on Dalia's inner wrist. But he had failed to consummate the ritual in time.

Wanting to make things easier on the beautiful human female who had turned his heart as easily as she had twisted his fate, Shelby had waited too long. And in doing so, he had created a lethal opportunity for one of the shadow descendants of Jaegar to get to Dalia first.

Valentine Nistor.

The true undead.

A living, breathing expression of evil itself.

As one of the oldest and more powerful of the Dark Vampires, Valentine had managed to take Shelby's life without ever lifting a finger—without ever drawing a single drop of blood.

Resentment stirred in Nathaniel's heart.

The Dark One was as cowardly as he was evil. He could have

fought like a warrior, but he had chosen to go after his enemy by manipulating the Blood Curse instead. A descendant of Jadon was a very hard creature to defeat in battle.

Nathaniel sighed and resolutely shut his eyes.

He was fighting to keep his tears at bay, struggling wildly against the rage that was mounting in his soul. A single tear escaped, and he quickly wiped it away.

What difference did it make? What had or hadn't happened to Dalia? The bottom line was the same: She had not given birth to Shelby's sons, and when the Blood Curse had come for the unnamed one, without the sacrifice of the darker twin to stay his sentence, Shelby had died an agonizing death of retribution. Punished for a crime he had never committed.

Nathaniel set his jaw in a hard line. He refused to engage in *what ifs* and *if onlys*—speculating about the ancient curse or wondering what Shelby's life would have been if the damnable thing no longer existed. The Blood Curse did exist. And it would always exist for his kind. As sure as the sun would always rise in the east and set in the west. Like all vampires, Nathaniel had simply learned to accept it. It was an intrinsic part of their way of life.

Kagen reached out and placed a steadying hand on Nathaniel's shoulder, his dark brown eyes focused on the ground. "You know I share your pain, brother." His voice was a mere whisper. "Like you, I have lived long enough to know the deeper tragedy of this loss. So many proud warriors gone…and for what?" He shook his head with disgust.

Nathaniel swayed, feeling suddenly light-headed. "I never thought it would hit this close to home. How could this have happened, Kagen? *To Shelby of all males?*"

"One word," Kagen said, "*Valentine*." He bit down on his lower lip, and his hand began to tremble. "But we cannot shed such tears, my brother. Remember, we must still guard our emotions."

Nathaniel knew his twin was right.

The force of such overwhelming grief spilling onto the earth from an ancient vampire could easily call forth an earthquake or command a flash flood. As it already stood, too many humans were going to die as a result of Shelby's passing, as a byproduct of the earth's grief.

Nathaniel nodded, his heart turning as cold and impassible as the stone slab his youngest brother now rested upon. He fisted his hands at his sides. Though he wanted to scream at the heavens, rage at the earth, weep until there were no tears left to cry, he knew he could not. His duty would not allow it.

His honor would not abide it.

Betraying no emotion whatsoever, he silently cursed his ancestors in the ancient tongue, daring them to retaliate, urging them to try and stake their claim on him before he could seek his vengeance for Shelby's death.

And he intended to seek his vengeance.

Kagen read Nathaniel's mind effortlessly. "You may not have a chance to impose your retribution, Warrior. Not if Marquis gets to the Dark One first."

Nathaniel glanced at his twin, noticing the subtle red embers glowing deep in the centers of his eyes. Kagen's own anger was scarcely contained.

"That might be true, brother, but if Marquis feels so strongly, then why isn't he here?"

"Nathaniel—"

"Do not excuse him, Kagen!"

Kagen shook his head. "I wasn't going to, brother."

Nathaniel sighed. "I know *exactly* what you were going to say, but that doesn't mean I understand…" His voice trailed off. "Nachari's absence? Sure. He couldn't possibly make it home in time, and Shelby's journey couldn't wait. But Marquis? He sits at home embracing the torment in his soul even as the shadows grow deeper within him. It isn't healthy. He needs to say good-bye."

Kagen frowned, his dark eyes filled with shared understanding. "You know he could not attend, Nathaniel. What did you expect him to do?" His voice held no hint of judgment. "The sky itself would have rained down blood and fire had Marquis been forced to place this blessed one in the ground. Marquis is too old. Too powerful. *Too angry*. I know he's always been the strong one, but I fear this may be too much…even for him."

Nathaniel rubbed his temples in slow, methodical circles, trying to ease some of his tension. Marquis was, indeed, having great difficulty with Shelby's death. "Has he spoken to you?"

"Briefly."

"And?"

"And he blames himself, Nathaniel. What do you think?"

Nathaniel shook his head. He knew that it was more than the injustice of the Blood Curse that tormented their ancient sibling, now fifteen hundred years old: Marquis was consumed with guilt over the *way* Shelby had died.

Kagen crossed his arms in front of him. "Marquis believes that the curse should have claimed him first. The Blood should have demanded a son from him long before it demanded one from Shelby. But it's the fact that Valentine got to Dalia—" He cut off his words the moment his voice began to quiver.

Nathaniel hissed beneath his breath. "None of us saw it coming."

"True." Kagen shifted uncomfortably. "But *Marquis* is the eldest, which makes him the sworn protector of our family. In his mind, he was responsible for the safety of his less powerful brother. As a male of honor, he should have seen to the safety of the human woman."

"It wasn't his mistake," Nathaniel insisted, knowing he felt guilty himself. "We all let Shelby down."

Kagen rubbed his eyes; he looked weary. "I know that. And Nachari knows that. But Marquis—"

"Will never forgive himself," Nathaniel supplied. He wiped his brow and shrugged his shoulders as if he could somehow lessen the weight of his grief with a gesture.

Kagen looked off into the distance. "Marquis will have to make his own peace with what happened in time."

Nathaniel hung his head. "Will you, Kagen? Will I?"

A long moment of silence passed between them before Kagen spoke again. "At any rate, Marquis is far too stubborn to take counsel from either of us. Perhaps Napolean can speak with him when things settle down…make him see that we are all equally to blame."

Maybe, Nathaniel thought. "He has to know that his leadership is still needed."

Kagen nodded. "More now than ever…" He cleared his throat. "Nachari should arrive tomorrow evening. Being Shelby's twin, he was even closer to him than the rest of us. He is definitely going to need Marquis's support."

Nathaniel agreed, although he couldn't imagine anything that would ease Nachari's pain. "Perhaps they can console each other…now that they each walk the world *as only one*."

The slip was inexcusable.

Nathaniel immediately averted his eyes and bowed his head in a slight nod of regret: a warrior's apology.

It was rare for a vampire to refer to the missing twin of the blood sacrifice. It was simply understood that in every family, there would always be an odd number of sons—an eldest brother who walked alone, the firstborn of light whose twin of darkness had been sacrificed at birth. It was seen as rude to mention the one who had never been named. Impolite to even acknowledge his existence.

Kagen overlooked Nathaniel's error. "This won't be easy for either of them. I do not look forward to all the dark days ahead of us."

"Nor do I."

Nathaniel stood up then and drew in a long, deep breath. "It is time," he whispered.

Kagen rose to his feet and slowly nodded.

With a wave of his hand, Nathaniel gradually began to lower the heavy stone slab deep into the earth, the body of his beloved brother resting silently upon it, uncovered, so that the earth would embrace him.

Nathaniel spoke softly in the ancient language of their ancestors, offering a prayer for peace—a final benediction—and then he requested *safe journey* to the Valley of Spirit and Light, making an impassioned plea to the Spirit of Jadon himself to grant Shelby absolution for his failure to relinquish a son.

Nathaniel watched helplessly as his cherished little brother descended deep into the ground, never to rise again. Despite his best efforts, two burning tears escaped his eyes, each one instantly transformed into a single heart-shaped diamond: the color, crimson red.

"Travel well, my brother. Go in peace."

∼

Jocelyn lifted the canteen from the weighty, navy blue backpack and took a long drink of water. She checked her compass once again, glancing furtively at the sky to determine the position of the sun. She was making great time. There was plenty of daylight left, more than enough to reach the cave before sunset. Placing the canteen back in the pack, she adjusted the weight evenly on her shoulders, her mind continuing to analyze information as she headed deeper into the forest.

Jocelyn knew that she didn't have permission to move on the tip her informant had given her. She wasn't supposed to be there. And if anything went wrong, she was on her own. But she also knew that it couldn't wait. *Human trafficking. Ritualistic killings.* The entire case was so bizarre.

As an agent of ICE, a highly specialized department within homeland security, Jocelyn Levi had been investigating one particularly shocking human-trafficking ring for months. Unlike more typical rings that forced young women into sexual slavery or sold children into forced labor, these victims were being taken for much darker purposes—to be used as sacrifices in ritualistic killings.

But by whom?

Jocelyn shook her head, carelessly tucking a handful of thick brown hair behind her ear. Over the last two months, her unit had discovered three freshly discarded bodies, each one showing signs of the same hideous brutality. The sight of the mutilated corpses had been abominable, but they were close to finding the head of the ring, or at least finding the man who was selling the women. Still, they had no idea who was doing the actual killings: what kind of cult could be behind such gruesome acts of evil. They had never managed to uncover an actual crime scene.

Jocelyn sighed, hoping that today would be a major breakthrough. If the information her source had given her about the cave was correct, then she was about to make a huge discovery.

Her informant had assured her that she was not walking into a danger zone, that the site he had told her about was no longer being used by the ring. As always, they changed locations frequently, moving around to avoid detection by the authorities. Unfortunately, this meant that there would be no fresh forensic evidence, but the information Jocelyn hoped to uncover was of a different kind anyway.

Jocelyn slowed her pace as a series of tall, reddish rock formations appeared in the distance, strangely shimmering into view like a desert mirage on a hot day. An eerie chill swept through her body, raising the hair on her arms, and a deep sense of foreboding settled into her stomach. She shivered and stared ahead. There was something about the peculiar canyons that shook her to her very core.

Although most people would have turned back, most people would not have been there in the first place.

Jocelyn was not most people.

Solving difficult crimes was her life. Stopping the *really, really* bad guys. And she was very good at it. She had always had a sixth sense, an uncanny ability to stay one step ahead of the criminal mind. It wasn't like she was psychic or anything. She just had a way of *feeling* things. Walking into a crime scene and *knowing*. As if the very essence of the place whispered secrets to her of the people who had been there.

Now, after months of dead ends, she finally had a reliable lead; and she had no intention of letting the information go to waste.

Jocelyn drew in a deep breath of crisp mountain air, her lungs working overtime to adjust to the altitude of the Eastern Rocky Mountains. The beautiful, expansive territory ran along the Front Range of North America, full of hidden canyons, dense forests, and towering, majestic peaks; under different circumstances, it might have been an idyllic place to vacation. Her sense of dread grew stronger with every step she took, so powerful that it almost felt as if there were an invisible hand holding her back, something warning her away. She shook her head in an effort to clear her mind as she pushed forward against the invisible barrier.

She had come way too far to turn back now.

The faces of the victims, their broken and tortured bodies, continued to replay in her mind like a gruesome, private slideshow, reminding her of just how much was at stake.

Picking up the pace, Jocelyn headed deeper into the canyon.

∽

The oddly shaped underground cavity, at the end of a series of narrow limestone tunnels, was exactly where Jocelyn's informant had said it would be: beneath a thin-arced entrance at the back of the cliffs, just beyond a waterfall. Jocelyn wondered how something so beautiful could be used for something so evil.

It was well after sunset when she reached the cavern.

She had slowly worked her way through a long labyrinth of passageways, going deeper into the earth with every step, until she had finally emerged in a gigantic chamber with enormous cathedral ceilings and jutting white columns. The scattered limestone pillars were erected haphazardly, as if a divine hand had simply tossed them about, and there was a small pond of stagnant water toward the back of the chamber, just beneath a series of low ledges. The cave itself was eerily dark, humid, and chilly. The air was musty and damp.

Jocelyn abruptly shut off her flashlight as a faint sound caught her attention. She thought she heard an echo coming from one of the adjoining tunnels. It sounded like a woman softly moaning.

She instinctively crouched down, her senses fully alert.

She reached for her gun, removed it from the holster, and ran to the rear of the cavern. Then she quietly waded through the sulfuric-smelling water, slid down onto her belly, and crawled like a snake beneath an extremely low rock overhanging. She repositioned her slender frame in the tight space so that she could still see out into the chamber, and burrowed in as deeply as possible.

God, I hope there are no spiders or bats in here, she silently prayed as the sound from the tunnel grew louder. Whoever was out there was clearly coming her way.

It was then that she saw the firelight erupt—as if on its own—illuminating the entire structure like a dark sky on the fourth of July.

Crude, ancient torches were anchored into the limestone walls in perfectly spaced increments, running all the way around the structure in a flawlessly level circle, and Jocelyn almost gasped as her eyes took in the details of the ancient cavern for the first time. Fiery orange blazes illuminated every nook and cranny of the chamber, revealing carefully carved structures placed purposefully throughout the room. It was an amazing circular fortress, no doubt created naturally by the earth over centuries of dissolution.

But it had also been carved by human hands into a ceremonial hall.

Jocelyn held her breath, hoping she was deep enough into the crevice not to cast a shadow into the stagnant water. For the first time, she noticed that there were three ledges spaced diametrically apart like the points of a triangle along the cavern walls, and each one led to a steep drop. A certain death should anyone try to escape.

The thought was bone chilling.

In the center of the room, there was a large stone slab with a smoothed surface, much like a bed made of granite, and there were intricate carvings on either side, ancient symbols that Jocelyn didn't recognize. But the color at the top of the stone was unmistakable. Jarring and unsettling. Jocelyn cringed as she imagined its purpose.

The center of the stone was a deep crimson red, the obvious result of years of decaying blood that had crystallized into the stone's pores. This was clearly not the work of a serial killer or a regional group of fanatics. This chamber was ancient. And these crimes were generational. The room spoke of a hidden way of life that had belonged to a people—*a culture*—for hundreds of years.

Adrenaline coursed through Jocelyn's body as the horror of the chamber sank in.

She held her breath and strained to see more.

On both sides of the bloodstained slab, there were additional man-made structures carved into granite: a raised altar on the left with a small basin smoothed into the top, and a wide bench on the right containing a backrest with arm-holds for comfort. Each structure sat about three feet away from the head of the slab.

Jocelyn shuddered.

She could feel the darkness and the unspoken pain etched into the fiber of the chamber, and once again, her stomach lurched. The hair on her arms stood up.

It was then that they entered.

A tall, dark, heavily muscled man. He was graceful yet intense, striking but dangerous. He was definitely malevolent.

Not human.

And he carried a very pregnant woman in his arms, obviously the one who had been moaning.

Dear God…

Jocelyn didn't know how she knew the creature wasn't human. She just knew. He looked like any other man, except that he was far too stunning, handsome in a way that seemed impossible. His long hair fell just below his shoulders in perfectly groomed waves, and his chiseled features were flawless, as if he were a statue rather than a man. But what really gave him away were his eyes. They were vacant…empty…soul-less.

Dark as the night and just as lifeless.

They might have held a strange beauty if they hadn't been so…dead.

And the color of his immaculate hair was unnatural too: It was a deep raven black, interspersed with bloodred tendrils, highlights that had not been added with dye. Jocelyn thought it shimmered like the surface of a lake beneath the moonlight; it was almost beautiful…in a demonic sort of way.

She hunkered lower and held her breath as she continued to watch, mesmerized.

The pregnant woman's eyes were open, but she looked unaware, like someone in a trance. She appeared to be young, maybe nineteen or twenty, with beautiful black hair and stunning green eyes. Her pale face was etched with…something…like a frozen look of terror from a nightmare. Thank God she was so checked out.

With a wave of his hand, the chamber began to fill with the smell of incense, and a dense gray fog began to hover just above the ground. It surrounded the bloodstained slab in the center of the room, instantly adding a ghostly feel to the chamber. Jocelyn couldn't scoot any further back into the crevice, so she tried to make herself smaller, willing her physical body to disappear.

There would be nothing she could do if he saw her.

Somehow, she knew, even as she cradled her gun in her hand, fully loaded and ready to fire, that her fate rested upon remaining hidden. There could be no detection. Luckily, the creature appeared far too engrossed with the pregnant woman to scan his surroundings, far too confident in his overwhelming power to concern himself with checking the chamber for others. And the sulfuric water she had waded through was a powerful mask of scent. Or at least she hoped it was.

There was a strange exhilaration gathering around him now. A sense of great expectation. Power radiated from the male as if it were seeping through his pores.

He glided to the bloodstained slab in the center of the chamber and slowly laid the woman down on the pallet. For a moment, Jocelyn thought she saw a hint of tenderness in his actions until she heard a faint laugh rise from deep within his throat. A twisted cross between a leopard's snarl and a hyena's hackling that made her skin crawl.

"Dalia, awaken," he commanded. His voice was like a velvet song, a rich cello from a concerto, as pure as the night and deeper than the ocean. He bent over the pregnant woman and kissed her. She awoke as commanded.

"Valentine, help me!"

She gulped the words in a desperate plea for mercy. Her eyes were wide with fright, and then, as she surveyed the chamber, a shriek of unbridled terror escaped her throat.

Jocelyn was not prepared for the sound that filled the cave.

The cry was so full of anguish that it momentarily stole her breath, even as it filled the room with electricity. It was unlike anything Jocelyn had ever heard before—the woman's misery was beyond comprehension.

Jocelyn had the sudden urge to vomit and had to struggle to

remain quiet as her stomach protested, threatening to give her presence away. Fortunately, the agonized screams drowned out the sound of her gagging.

The woman was in labor, and something was terribly wrong.

She writhed and screamed. Tried frantically to crawl away. But the man simply leaned over her, watching with indifference as he placed one powerful hand against her chest, pressed her down, and held her to the stone.

Jocelyn shook her head and blinked several times, as if trying to wake up from a nightmare, hoping it was all a bad dream.

The pain continued.

The torture persisted.

The cries went on for what seemed an eternity, sweat pouring from the woman's forehead, her hands clenched in a contortion of anguish, as the dark male sat quietly watching the whole scene with a look of pleasure gleaming in his eyes.

The man shifted back and forth on the hard bench.

He appeared to be deliberately controlling his breathing, and there was an erotic quality to his movement. It was as if he were deriving sexual pleasure from the woman's suffering, struggling to restrain himself from touching her while she labored.

Unable to bring his excitement under control, he bent over and pressed a hard kiss against her mouth as she moaned in pain. It was beyond sociopathic.

And then, what happened next was so shocking that it left Jocelyn both hypnotized and repulsed at the same time: The creature's perfect lips drew back like a predator's snarl, and his canine teeth slowly lengthened into two razor-sharp…*fangs*. And then he scraped them back and forth over the woman's neck—again and again—leaving deep, jagged gashes in his wake. Groaning in a low growl of ecstasy, he finally sank them deep into her flesh, his body shuddering with pleasure as she cried out in pain.

The entire scene was unspeakably brutal. Jocelyn felt like time was standing still as she lay motionless on the floor of the cave, desperate to conceal her own presence from the monster.

Helpless to save the suffering woman.

And then the woman's struggle reached a fevered pitch. Her cries grew so forlorn that Jocelyn actually considered drawing her weapon and revealing her own presence just to end her suffering.

There was no time.

Muscles began to stretch. Bones cracked and ribs popped. As a terror that could only be described as unholy rose in the form of a plaintive wail from the woman's throat. The baby was not moving down through the birth canal, but up...*up*...into the chest cavity. Jocelyn fought to hold back her own terrified scream, and her mouth fell open in horror as the woman's rib cage exploded outward. Fragmenting as it burst open, it exposed her heart and lungs.

The dark creature sighed in contentment.

He stood up over the broken body, reached into the gaping cavity, and lifted out what appeared to be *two* perfect newborn infants—both males—with thick, raven black hair. Hair striped with demonic strands of crimson red.

When the creature strolled to the raised altar, he seemed to falter for the first time, like he was struggling to remain in control. He placed the firstborn of the two sons gently into the basin, pausing only long enough to stare into the child's eyes and place a soft kiss on his forehead. It was as if he knew he couldn't keep the child. The tenderness was bizarre.

Instinctively, he held the remaining infant close to his chest and moved back from the altar. He watched the abandoned baby squirm, and his eyes became as cold as ice.

The dark fog moved then.

It swirled, becoming increasingly solid and thick.

It took the form of two long arms with extended, skeletal fingers as it reached and grasped. Moaned and wailed. In a shrill, high-pitched cry of victory.

The wail became louder as the fog swirled closer to the altar, where the child lay waiting.

And then Valentine's muscles clenched. His forehead wrinkled with tension. And his gaze became a fiery red ember of loathing as he watched the fog approach the child.

Yet, he didn't move a muscle as the grayish-black mist surrounded the crying infant. As it reached out to tighten its ghostly fingers around the newborn's neck…

Then just like that—the child was gone.

Valentine growled a low, angry snarl, his powerful frame trembling with rage, and then he simply turned away, lifted the remaining child high in the air, and smiled, a twisted grin exposing his perfect white teeth.

"You shall be named Derrian," he declared in a deep, resounding voice. "And now the Blood Curse shall never claim me. I am forever immortal." A wicked smirk crossed his face. "While Shelby Silivasi—*the beloved descendant of Jadon*—is forever dead."

He spat the words sarcastically, his laughter echoing all the way to the high cathedral ceilings.

"And this woman…" he gestured toward the stone where Dalia lay dead, her eyes still open wide in horror, "was truly a waste of a beautiful body, don't you think?"

He laughed again and held the newborn baby to his soul-less heart.

Waving a carefree hand over Dalia, he sent the tortured body up in flames, cremating her as he sauntered out of the chamber.

Softly singing a lullaby to his son.

～

Jocelyn raced frantically across the winding mountain path. She ran with all the speed she could muster, dirt and rocks kicking up behind her as her feet left the ground. The limbs of nearby trees reached out to scratch her skin when she got too close. Her heart pounded uncontrollably as images of the horror she had witnessed replayed in her mind.

She had waited in the dark cavern long after midnight, wanting to be sure the creature was gone before she attempted to make an escape. Taking only her identification from her backpack, she had placed her gun safely in its holster over her right shoulder and flung the half-full canteen of water over her left. Then, she had hastily thrown the heavy pack over one of the steep drops before sprinting wildly through the dark maze of tunnels in a frenzied effort to get out of the cave.

Jocelyn fell several times in her hasty escape, bruising and scraping her knees, but she barely felt any pain as her adrenaline carried her miles through the forest.

When she finally stopped to rest, her lungs labored for breath, even as her mind cried out for sanity. *It couldn't be!* What she had seen could not be real. What kind of creature was that?

And the poor, helpless woman...

How could anyone suffer such a heartless death?

Jocelyn bent over, panting heavily. Her hands were on her knees, and she fought to take in oxygen in the high, unforgiving altitude. She struggled to clear her usually organized mind.

Dalia.

The murdered woman.

Had she been one of the victims sold into slavery by the ring? Had that creature purchased her...*to breed*? To murder? Had he kept her for nine whole months? And if so, what in God's name had that poor woman endured?

Most of the women involved in the ring she had been investigating were foreigners. Poor, unsuspecting immigrants forced to trust the wrong person in a desperate attempt to come to the United States. But Dalia had been American. At least she had looked American. And she had sounded American, too, when she had spoken the creature's name.

Valentine.

Jocelyn shuddered and blinked back a reservoir of pressing tears. The woman in the chamber had been beautiful. And she had suffered unbearably.

Jocelyn could not get far enough away…fast enough. She took a few more labored breaths, then forced herself to get moving again. She tried to keep up a steady jog even though her lungs felt like they were on fire. Her mind continued to piece the puzzle together as she ran…

What kind of a creature started fires with the wave of his hand? Who held down a struggling adult woman—pregnant or not—with only the tips of his fingers? *Whose children emerged from the body like alien beings as opposed to being born in the natural way?*

And the blood.

He drank blood.

Jocelyn tried to convince herself that he was just some sort of incredibly strong, psychopathic killer. Maybe a crazed addict pumped up on drugs, someone who had given himself so completely over to darkness that he no longer had a conscience. But she knew better. As impossible as it was, Jocelyn knew the truth: That thing was *undead*. Wholly evil. Dangerous beyond measure and definitely not human.

That thing was a *vampire*.

Even as the prospect settled in her mind, it was hard to accept it as true.

The narrow, uneven path beneath her feet was littered with branches, scattered with pine cones, and strewn with raised tree roots. The loose soil formed uneven divots beneath her feet, causing her to trip and fall far too often, having only a flashlight for a guide. The enormous gathering of shadowed, towering pines, interspersed with quaking aspens, gave the forest a haunted appearance.

As if it were bursting with mystical beings. All of them lurking.

Towering over and around her. Hiding just out of sight. Crouched and ready to pounce as she ran by.

Every shadow was a ghost. Every sound was the creature finding her. Every whisper was a vampire waiting to claim her.

Jocelyn put her hands over her ears. She could feel the desperate pounding in her head even as she tried to control her thoughts and keep her eyes focused on the path ahead of her.

One step at a time, she coaxed. *Just keep going one step at a time.*

A large, jutting tree root caught her ankle as she rounded a sharp curve in the path, just as a wolf howled from somewhere deep in the forest. The tree felt like two evil hands snatching her legs, and she was certain the howl was an insidious snarl, that the vampire had found her and was about to take her to his lair. She screamed a hair-raising shriek of terror as her knees struck the ground and her hands flew out in front of her to catch her fall. She clenched her eyes shut and trembled uncontrollably.

She was too afraid to open them.

Too afraid to move.

So gripped with terror she was paralyzed.

She huddled close to the ground, trying desperately to regain her composure.

As long as she lived, she would never get over what had happened in that chamber. No matter how tightly she held her hands over her ears, she couldn't shut out the echo of those anguished cries. Now, miles away from the bloody cavern, Jocelyn finally began to feel—not just to analyze or survive—but to deeply, intrinsically feel the full horror of what she had seen.

Like the rising tide of an ocean wave, the anguish swelled in her heart, and she began to sob. She gathered her knees to her chest, buried her face in her hands, and rocked back and forth while she wept.

Jocelyn Levi cried uncontrollably, maintaining a far too fragile hold on her sanity.

A SNEAK PEEK FROM DRAGONS REALM

(BOOK #1 – DRAGONS REALM SAGA)

Mina Louvet was only twelve years old the day she was taken by the Dragons Guard, the day she was ripped from her mother's arms in order to be schooled in the ways of the Ahavi, those who would serve the Dragon. She had been chosen for her aptitude in linguistics, her burgeoning ability to speak multiple languages, both those of ancient tongues and foreign lands, and for her rare, almond-shaped eyes.

She had been chosen because Wavani, the king's witch, had assured the king that Mina would one day be one of the few, the chosen, the Sklavos Ahavi, a female who could not only bear healthy children but would *only give birth to sons*. The witch had seen it in a Seeking Vision, and the revelation had been enough to change Mina's life forever.

Now, at the age of eighteen, Mina, along with two other *chosen* females, entered Castle Dragon for the first time. As she stepped into the grand receiving hall, she had to will herself to be strong, to hold her head up with pride, to keep her shoulders from slumping in defeat. She had to consciously keep her knees from knocking together in fright.

Her eyes darted around the enormous foyer in anxious, furtive glances, as she gawked at the numerous examples of opulent wealth: The architecture was cutting-edge and grandiose. The artwork was rare, refined, and priceless. And the floor beneath her feet was made of exquisite marbled stone, reflecting the purest blue veins and pearlescent arroyos Mina had ever seen.

The ceiling was beyond magnificent. It must have stood at least fifty feet high and, heavily coffered in ornate tiles, its large uncut beams framed the massive structure like a celestial curtain. And the sparse but ornate furnishings—the round table by the grand entry; the golden wing-back chairs, placed on either side of the enormous staircase; the pair of vintage, velvet sofas that sat up against the textured walls—they all looked too elegant to touch, too expensive to sit upon. This was the Dragons' home. The castle where King Demitri once lived with his infamous Queen Kalani, a Sklavos Ahavi who, prior to her death, had given the king four noble sons: one who had died by his own hand, and three, still living, who would remain in the gigantic fortress to serve the Realm along with their newly acquired Ahavi.

At least until the Autumn Mating.

For once the sons were wed, they would be sent out into the three rural provinces, along with Mina, Tatiana, and Cassidy, to set up their own royal courts and rule as dragons of old.

A soft echo accompanied a dainty set of footfalls as Pralina Darcy, the Ahavis' governess, descended the grand staircase, rounded the corner into the foyer, and strode regally before the girls, her head held high enough to intersect with low-lying clouds. "Welcome to Castle Dragon," she said in a cocky drawl. "This will be your new home for the next five months, and I will be your mistress."

Mina swallowed a lump in her throat and glanced longingly over her shoulder at the main castle doorway. She had half a mind to take off running, to dart beneath the high wooden arches, dash into the nearby woods, and escape the boundaries of the Realm forever.

She wanted another reality.

She wanted another life.

She pressed her palm against her lower belly and curtsied instead. "Governess."

Pralina began to walk in slow, demeaning circles around the cluster of girls, her face a mask of disinterest. She appraised the group much like a common farmer might appraise a herd of cows at market, studying their features, scrutinizing their figures, and assessing their postures with barely concealed disdain. And then she reached out to grab a lock of Mina's raven-black hair. "Do you shampoo with rose water?"

Mina nearly teetered in place. "I…I…yes…sometimes."

Pralina frowned, her severe gray eyes reflecting dubious shadows in their depths. "You stutter?"

Mina shrank back. "N…no, ma'am. I'm just nervous."

Pralina bent low to Mina's ear. "Do not stutter in the presence of the dragons."

Mina nodded, unable to reply, unwilling to risk another misstep.

Pralina let go of her hair and stepped to the side, evaluating Tatiana next. "Your name?"

The shy girl winced and averted her eyes. "Tatiana Ward." Her voice was barely audible.

Pralina fingered the high, lacy neckline of Tatiana's gown and scowled in reproach. "Are you a prude, uneasy, or just stupid? You cover your shoulders, your breasts, and your throat…on *this* day?"

When Tatiana started to tremble, Mina wanted to reach out and slap Pralina across the face, governess or not. Of course they were all nervous and uneasy—who wouldn't be? They were the future brides of dragons, glorified slaves, offered like lambs to the slaughter for the supposed good of the Realm. And even if that had not been the case, Tatiana would not have been well suited for this duty. She was unbearably shy, far too sensitive, and this heartless woman, this prickly governess, was nothing more than a bully—*as if they didn't have enough to fret over already.*

Mina bit her bottom lip in an effort to hold her tongue. She watched as Tatiana curled inward, her frail frame retreating like a tortoise's head inside of a shell, and thought about how hard the girl had struggled at the Keep, how deeply Tatiana had grieved her inescapable destiny.

Like Mina, Tatiana Ward had been born to a common family in the poorest province, only Tatiana's family had desperately needed her help on the farm. Unfortunately, that fact had not mattered at all to the Dragons Guard or the imperious king—not one iota. Once Wavani had discovered that Tatiana was a Sklavos Ahavi, her significance as anything more than a servant to the Realm, a future bearer of a dragon's sons, had been completely disregarded. It was as if her value as a person no longer mattered, as if she were nothing more than a commodity to be traded.

Mina sighed, understanding it all too well.

Even as a child, Mina had been a rare beauty: Her long, raven hair fell in thick, glossy waves down her gracefully sloped back, the silky tresses a flawless complement to her deep green eyes; and her uncanny ability with languages, her miraculous ability to memorize and understand foreign dialects, had ultimately sealed her fate. The fact that another rare beauty, Tatiana Ward, had also excelled in economics, that she understood the complex dynamics of running a royal treasury and seemed to just *get* the finer nuances of a ledger, had rendered any possible objection to her service futile. With ringlet, auburn curls and soft, amber eyes, Tatiana was stunning, plain and simple. She was a fiscal asset to the Realm, and her body was ripe to bear sons. The fact that she was painfully shy and far too delicate to withstand the lustful, temperamental demands of a dragon simply didn't matter to the powers around her. And that fact, that harsh reality, had been a devastating blow to Tatiana's family and, quite frankly, a cruel twist of fate Tatiana didn't deserve.

None of them did, really.

Well, except, *perhaps*, for Cassidy.

Even before Pralina could approach the obnoxious female, Cassidy took a bold step forward. She flipped her shoulder-length blond hair, batted her crystal-blue eyes, and angled her jaw in defiance. "I am Cassidy Bondeville."

Pralina drew back in surprise. "Did I ask you to speak?"

Cassidy manufactured a frown as severe as Pralina's. "No, ma'am. You did not." Her voice was clipped and brazenly unapologetic.

Pralina raised her open palm and held it just inches from Cassidy's jaw. For a moment, Mina could have sworn the governess was going to slap her, but then, as the tension slowly ebbed, she stroked the side of Cassidy's rosy cheek with her thumb, instead. "Ah yes, Cassidy Bondeville, born to a high-bred family in the common province. Eager to get on with it, I see."

Cassidy shrugged her shoulders with haughty indifference. "Eager *enough*...to serve the Realm."

Pralina snorted. "I see: *to serve the Realm*." She laughed out loud, and then she took several steps back and regarded all three girls circumspectly. "As Cassidy has so humbly reminded us all"—she spat the word *humbly* with heavy sarcasm—"you are here to serve the Realm." She snickered. "More importantly, you are here to serve the king. More *specifically*, you are here to learn what you must over the next five months in order to *serve* Damian, Dante, or Drake Dragona however they see fit." She cleared her throat and smiled, and it was a wicked parody of mirth. "When the leaves turn color in autumn, which they inevitably will, the witch will make her recommendations to the king. Those recommendations, along with whatever petitions His Majesty receives from his sons, will ultimately determine your fate, which one of you will be bound to each dragon son. You have no say in the matter, and if you were not already fit for this appointment, you wouldn't be here. It is my job to make you *worthy* before then, to ensure your absolute obedience. It is your job to comply."

Tatiana choked back a sob, and Mina reached out to take her hand, hoping to provide whatever comfort she could. "Ignore her," she whispered beneath her breath. "She's just trying to scare us." She left out the fact that it was working.

Tatiana squeezed Mina's hand in desperation, and Mina responded in kind.

It was the wrong thing to do.

Pralina instantly stiffened and glared crossly at Mina. "What did you just say to that girl…a moment ago?"

"Nothing, Governess. I just—"

Pralina seized Mina by the arm and dug her nails into her flesh. She squeezed so hard that her bony fingers drew blood, and then she slapped Tatiana's linked hand away. "You just told this girl to ignore me. Are you insane?"

"No," Mina said, realizing she should stop there but unable to hold her tongue a moment longer. "I didn't tell her to ignore *you*. I told her to ignore your flagrant attempt at intimidation, your obvious need to humiliate us." She clasped one hand over Pralina's, unpeeled the bony fingers from her bleeding arm, and met the governess's icy stare head-on. "I told her you were just trying to scare us." This time, she didn't stutter.

Pralina drew in a sharp, angry breath. "You willful, insolent…*whore*! Do you not know that I could have the flesh peeled back from your bones, have that tongue cut out of your insolent mouth? There are dozens of Ahavi at the Keep just waiting for the opportunity to take your place. Do you think you are irreplaceable, you stupid, rebellious wench?"

Mina clenched her fists and her arms began to tremble. She was *this close* to taking a swing at Pralina's jaw when the room suddenly grew cold, and the air grew inexplicably still. It was as if someone had thrown open a window in a dark, creepy attic and a glacial mist had swept into the room. As the eerie, otherworldly wind swirled about the foyer, a tall, imposing male stepped out of the fog.

Great ghosts of the original dragons, Mina thought. This was not someone to toy with.

The male had to be at least six-foot-two, and he was dressed in form-fitting breeches and a silk black shirt, one that bore the unmistakable emblem of the dragon in the upper left corner. The royal sigil was a deep blood red; the dragon itself was embroidered in gold; and in the center of the dragon's eye, just below his angry brow, there was a polished inset diamond. It was roughly cut and blazing with light. In fact, it almost appeared alive, as if it were waiting...and watching...guarding the dragon's heart.

The male was just as cryptic.

His angular features were drawn so taut they appeared to be chiseled in stone, and he practically glided when he walked, slinking forward in the most inhuman manner. His muscles contracted and released in waves, rising like the haunches of a predatory cat, descending like an ocean's foam, as his rich onyx hair shifted in the preternatural breeze, cascading around his proud, broad shoulders. Power radiated from his hidden aura; danger settled in his wake; and all the while, his midnight-blue eyes shone like dark sapphires, emerging from hidden flames.

His movement, *his very essence*, was chilling yet deceptively calm.

He was utterly terrifying in his animal grace.

Pralina stepped back and bowed her head, and for a moment, Mina thought about doing the same. Heck, she thought about climbing underneath the nearest piece of furniture, but she stood, transfixed, watching Pralina's obedient, submissive behavior.

It reminded her of a pack of wolves she had observed while living at the Keep.

It had been the dead of winter, and she had been gathering wood in the forest when she came across an alpha, a pack leader, snarling at a beta pup. The pup had tucked in his tail, bent back his ears, and exposed his underbelly in submission, much like Pralina was doing right now.

Mina shivered.

The governess's body language was more than acquiescent—it was positively withdrawn. "Milord." Pralina spoke the word with *reverence* and more than a little fear.

The male spared her a glance and waited.

For what?

Mina had no idea.

But the seconds seemed like hours as the bizarre scene dragged on. And then, all at once, realization dawned on her: This wasn't about Pralina or her piteous show of submission. It was about the royal prince reining in his beast. Somehow, Mina just knew he was telling his barely leashed, primordial instincts to heel, that he was commanding himself *not* to hurt the governess.

And then, just like that, his countenance softened.

He shrugged his shoulders and inclined his head, casually regarding all three girls without meeting their eyes. "Governess…" His voice was laced with unspoken command.

"My prince?"

He gestured toward the Sklavos Ahavi. "Name them."

Pralina nodded far too enthusiastically, and her tongue darted out to lick her quivering lips. "As you wish, milord." She pointed at Mina first. "My prince, Dante: This is Mina Louvet, from the southern province. She is renowned for her aptitude with foreign languages and her knowledge of distant cultures." She turned her attention to the shy beauty quaking in her boots. "Tatiana Ward is also from the *commonlands*. Although she hails from a poor family, she is now well-educated and shows great promise in mathematics and commerce. I believe she is the most obedient of the three." She cut her eyes at Mina as she spoke the previous phrase, and then she immediately turned her attention to Cassidy. "And Cassidy Bondeville is from a well-bred family, wealthy and respected. She is eager to serve the Realm."

Dante listened, but he kept his eyes averted, his head cocked slightly to the side.

He didn't look at any of them.

He simply nodded after each introduction, and then, without saying a word, he silently turned on his heels and strolled to the castle doors.

The dismissal—*the absolute disregard and ownership*—was as glaring as his silence and far more foreboding.

Both gave Mina the chills.

She watched as he walked away, both silent and proud, without bothering to look back or even dismiss the governess, and something inside of her recoiled.

Mina didn't know what she had expected, what she had hoped would happen the first time she laid eyes on a dragon, but this wasn't it: Perhaps she had expected an interrogation or a sharp, condescending diatribe, outlining exactly what was expected of each girl, what would and would not be tolerated. Perhaps she had expected the dragon to snarl when he spoke or to radiate cruelty with his eyes, to regard them with hostility or disdain, even vulgar innuendo—after all, they were *his* to do with as he pleased—but this, this casual disregard and quiet dismissal, it was truly beyond the pale. After six long years of servitude—living, working, and training in utter desolation at the Keep—after nearly a decade as nothing more than a ward of the state, Mina had expected something more.

Anything.

More.

Somehow, Mina had at least expected to be acknowledged as alive.

Just then, Dante turned around in the doorway, and his severe eyes met *hers*. It was as if he had heard her thoughts—was that even possible?

"Mina..." His voice was hardly more than a whisper. "There are two horses saddled in the courtyard, a black stallion and a white gelding. The stallion is my personal steed; the gelding is now yours. Take your mount." His voice was as enchanting as the night sky and just as dark. He didn't await a reply. He simply sauntered out the doors.

Mina's stomach turned over in sudden waves of nausea, and she locked her gaze on Tatiana's—the girl's face was positively ashen—before turning her attention to Pralina. "Governess?"

Pralina scowled. "Go, girl."

Mina winced. She looked down at her attire—she was wearing a calf-length, flowing tunic of emerald green and opal white over a tight-fitting undergarment that hugged her hips, thighs, and legs. "Should I not change first?" *Dearest goddess of light*, what did Dante want with her? Had he truly overheard her private thoughts? And if so, what then? Or had he actually overheard her prior insolence with Pralina before he entered the room? Was he going to take her into the woods and dispose of her?

Or worse?

"I...I don't understand."

Pralina took a menacing step forward, her frigid body drawing so close to Mina's that their noses almost touched. "Which part of this is giving you pause? Your *lord* has given you a command. *Go.*"

Mina swallowed her apprehension and nodded. This was what she had wanted, right? To be acknowledged as alive? Suddenly, the idea seemed utterly preposterous: Dante Dragona, the firstborn son of King Demitri and Queen Kalani, was a dragon, a supernatural being with untold power, no matter how human he seemed. The last thing Mina wanted was to be alone with him.

She clutched the leather pouch around her neck, an amulet given to her by her mother before she was taken to the Keep: It contained a lock of her mother's hair, a likeness of her sister, Raylea, drawn by her father on an aged piece of parchment, and the petals of a tulip, one Mina had grown as a child in the family's humble garden; and it usually gave her strength.

Usually.

Today was altogether different.

"Of course," she finally mumbled, feeling more than a little bit queasy. Gathering her courage, she headed for the door.

∽

Mina forced herself to place one foot in front of the other, to simply keep her eyes on the cobblestone path before her, as she stoically made her way toward the white horse. A deep, guttural sound brought her up short—*was that actually a growl?*—and her eyes shot to Dante. She took an unwitting step backward. "Milord?"

"You're bleeding." He licked his full lips before waving her forward with his hand. "Come to me."

Mina's heart began to race in her chest. She glanced down at her wounded arm and quickly covered it with the palm of her other hand. "It's…it's nothing."

His voice dropped to a sultry purr, devastating in its intensity. "I said, *come to me.*"

Mina gulped. She raised her chin, took a slow, deep breath, and tentatively stepped forward.

"Closer."

She took another step forward. And then, with a wave of impatience, Dante narrowed his eyes on her feet, his pupils flashed burnt orange or crimson—it was too fast to tell—and she was suddenly standing before him, their toes nearly touching. *Blessed Nuri, Lord of Fire, the dragon had moved her body with his mind.* She quickly dismissed the thought; it was more than she could grasp.

"What happened?" he asked, as he reached out to take her arm.

Mina fought not to pull it away and tuck it behind her back. "Nothing."

He smiled faintly, but there was no joy in the expression. "Six years at the Keep and you still do not understand authority?"

She assumed the question was rhetorical, but she answered anyway. "No…I mean *yes*…milord." She watched him as he studied the wounds on her arm.

"I'll ask again: *What happened?*"

"Pralina," Mina whispered. When he glared at her angrily, she added, "She snatched my arm and dug her nails into my flesh."

"Why?"

"I…because…in response to my insolence." She bit her bottom lip.

He nodded. *"Pralina…"* And then he began to caress the wound absently with his thumb. He rubbed slow circles over the jagged incisions as he studied them more closely, and then he pressed his own thumbnail into the deepest of the cuts.

"Ouch!" Mina flinched.

"Shh, be still," he whispered, and then he did something as strange as it was unexpected. He slowly bent his head, his midnight hair falling forward in a silken frame that shielded his eyes, and lapped up the blood in three slow strokes of his tongue.

Mina gasped. She drew back her arm and stared at him in morbid fascination. She looked down at her arm and shuddered—the wounds were all gone.

He gestured toward the horse. "Your mount, Mina."

Mina took a courageous step toward the beautiful white gelding and reached for the sloped leather horn, and then she froze.

She had thought she could do this.

Heck, she had been trained for six long years to do *just this*, but the reality of the Dragons—the reality of Dante—was far more foreboding than she had expected. Nothing she had been taught had prepared her for this first real-life encounter, the overwhelming presence of the preternatural male standing so close beside her, the way he watched her with *those eyes*, the way he appraised her with barely concealed ferocity in his gaze. And she wasn't at all sure she could go through with it, that she wouldn't end up being executed for disobedience before the encounter was over.

She reached once more for the saddle horn, willing her body to comply with the prince's command. After all, what was the big deal? How hard was it to go for a ride on horseback? She was as sure in the saddle as anyone—all the Sklavos Ahavi were—they were trained to be so. Just the same, her hand trembled, and she could barely remain steady on her feet. She released the saddle horn and wiped her sweaty hand along the front of her tunic. "Where are you taking me?" she asked, hoping to distract him while she regained her composure.

Dante measured her thoughtfully. He glanced at the horse, assessed her trembling hands, and then looked off into the distance, as if giving her a moment to collect her wits. "I am going to show you the castle grounds, the land around the settlement, and you are going to commit it to memory."

Mina nodded. That sounded innocent enough. "Why?" she whispered. "I mean, *why me?*" She waited with bated breath.

Dante grew motionless, far too still, and he stood like that, like a granite statue, for what seemed like an eternity before reaching out to take her by the arm and spin her around to face him. "Look at me, Ahavi."

Mina looked up into his bottomless dark eyes and almost faltered. His face was haunting in its perfection yet terrifying in its subtle brutality. There was something unidentifiable lurking just beneath the surface of those eyes, something ancient, wise, and *deadly*. They held fire and ice; war and blood; passion and pain in their depths.

Power beyond imagining.

Mina tore her gaze from Dante's and studied his features instead: His cheeks were chiseled, as if in stone, the harsh, unyielding angles just *shy* of cynical and cruel. His nose was straight and noble, sculpted at the tip as if by the hands of an artisan, and his brows were perfectly arched, not too straight, not too thin…not too full. His chin was strong; his mouth was sultry; and his skin was as smooth as the day he was born. *Do dragons age?* she wondered. *How long do they really live?* Legend had it that they were nearly immortal, and if that were the case, what would become of her, Tatiana, and Cassidy as they grew older?

Again, the thought was too unsettling to ponder, so she dismissed it.

Forcing herself to meet his steely gaze, she asked, "Are you going to answer me?" She wished her mouth would just stay *shut*.

Dante held her gaze, unblinking, until she finally turned away. And then, he raised his right hand to touch her nose with his index finger, a light tap on the tip of her flesh. "Don't ever question me like that again, Mina." His voice was cold and uncompromising. "You may ask questions if you're curious, but don't ever insist upon an answer."

Mina's eyes grew wide. Oh, *hell's fire*, she knew better. What was happening to her? Her knees grew weak in fear of retaliation. "Forgive me," she whispered, not so much because she regretted breaking the rules, but because she understood all too well just who *and what* he was. She closed her eyes. "Apologies, milord."

He clasped her by the chin and gently tilted her head upward. "Open your eyes."

She obeyed, half expecting him to strike her.

"Beautiful," he whispered, slowly releasing his hold. "Now then: I am taking you on a ride around the grounds so that you will know which areas are safe and which are forbidden. I will show you the best places to find fruit…and flowers…and the best places to hide should the fortress be attacked."

Mina's head was spinning, her thoughts swirling around like rain in a nor'easter wind. *He wanted to show her where to find fruit…and flowers…and where to hide?* What was he? A lover or a sadist? She stood, motionless, waiting for him to continue.

"As for *why you?*" He rubbed his chin thoughtfully. "Because you are the Sklavos Ahavi I have chosen for my mate."

A SNEAK PEEK FROM DRAGONS REALM

Mina's mouth dropped open. She tried to gather her thoughts, but her fear got the best of her. *Was he kidding?* What did he mean *he had chosen her as his mate?* It was way too soon! He hadn't even looked at the other girls in the foyer. In fact, he knew nothing about her beyond Pralina's initial introduction. And besides, the witch, Wavani, had to make the final recommendations. "The choice is your father's," she blurted in a rush, "the king's." Oh great goddess of mercy, she could not be wed to this fearsome creature.

Dante smiled lazily, his countenance unperturbed. "Mm, perhaps that is true, but I am the king's firstborn. He will respect my wishes."

Mina gasped. "But you just met me! You haven't even spoken with Tatiana or Cassidy yet."

Dante reached out to twirl a lock of her hair through his rugged fingers, and he sighed. "Your hair is like mine, as dark as the midnight sky." He ran his thumb along the side of her jaw. "Your eyes are the color of emeralds, as rare as they are exquisite." He clasped his hands behind his back and studied her from head to toe, without apology. "You are beautiful," he whispered, "and our sons will be strong."

Mina gasped and took a step back, grasping at straws. "But… but…" The words wouldn't come.

He placed his open palm against her heart, his thumb settling far too close to her breast. "And you have fire in your soul, Mina Louvet. More than enough to feed a hungry dragon."

Mina tried to remember her place, to restrain from removing Dante's hand from her chest—*she really did*—but the terror was beginning to overwhelm her. Brushing his hand aside, she held both palms up to usher him back. "Please, my prince. Don't touch me like that." She felt her body begin to tremble, and she might have given vent to tears if she hadn't been so deeply opposed to giving him the satisfaction.

She waited quietly then…

To die.

Dante stared at her with a disapproving gaze, but there was no hint of retribution in his eyes. His brows didn't furrow, and his jaw didn't stiffen. He didn't grow scales or fangs. Only, his eyes, those glorious, dangerous eyes; they glowed with the reflection of flames in the centers, a dragon's fire barely restrained. "Take your mount, Mina," he growled, turning away to gather his stallion's reins.

Mina exhaled in relief, stunned that she was still standing. Still breathing.

Loosely grabbing the reins, she reached for the horn on her saddle, set a foot in the stirrup, and started to hoist herself up. Yet, and again, her trembling grew unmanageable. Cursing herself for her weakness, she froze where she perched and simply tried to take in air, one breath in, one breath out. *"Inhale deeply, Mina, then release it,"* she whispered beneath her breath.

Dante was instantly behind her, his massive frame towering above hers. He placed one hand on either side of her waist, pressed his chest blatantly against her back, and bent to her ear. "Relax, Ahavi. The beast can smell your fear."

Mina looked up at her horse. He was beginning to snort and prance in place, and she knew her emotions had transferred to the intuitive animal. She shook her head to clear the cobwebs. "*Of course.* I don't mean to frighten the horse. I'll try—"

Dante rested his chin on the crown of her head. He nuzzled her hair and sighed, his body growing noticeably tense. "I wasn't referring to the horse."

Mina dropped the reins. She quickly stepped to the side, eyed the pasture just beyond the courtyard, and then, without thinking or reasoning, she took off running, her legs moving faster than they had ever moved before. Her arms pumped furiously and her lungs burned like fire as she glanced repeatedly over her shoulder, awaiting the dragon's pursuit.

Dante stood by the horses and watched as she placed more and more distance between them. He didn't call out to her, and he didn't shift into whatever form a dragon took. He simply watched her run as if she were putting on a show for his amusement.

Finally, he said something to the animals—as if they could understand him?—and began to walk in her direction.

Mina picked up the pace, frantic to get away.

She scanned the surrounding fields, searching for a place to hide, while Dante just kept walking.

When, at last, she reached the edge of the woods, he made his move.

He jumped.

Or flew.

Whatever it was, she couldn't be certain, but it propelled him forward at enormous speed.

Dante Dragona was no longer a man, yet he wasn't a dragon, either. He was simply a blur of motion, an impression of light, traveling faster than time or space should allow, hurtling toward her with lethal purpose. "Stop!" The force of his voice brought her up short as surely as if he had bound her hands and feet in a pair or iron shackles.

Mina tugged against the invisible binds, the mystical power that held her in place like an unseen hand. "Release me," she pleaded.

"Be still," he barked.

Mina struggled mightily against...*against*...against what? She was desperate to break free. "Please, Dante. I can't do this. I don't know how to do this."

"To do what?" He encircled her from behind, again. Only, this time, he clamped his powerful arms around her waist and pulled her back against him, the tops of both hands brushing indecently against the sides of her breasts. "Do what?" he repeated. "This?" He tightened his hold.

"Yes," Mina cried. *"Please."*

"Please, what?" he repeated.

She ceased her struggles. "Please, let go."

He bit her on the neck, just between the juncture of her throat and her collarbone, and his teeth felt much sharper than they looked. He held her like that, like a lion restraining a cub, until at last she froze beneath him, and he let go. "You will not question me, Mina," he growled. "You will not tell me when I may touch you and when I may not."

Mina grimaced. She tugged at his hands to no avail. "It's *my* body, milord."

"No," he whispered coldly. "It is not. It is mine."

Mina could hardly believe her ears. "But you haven't even considered Tatiana or Cassidy. All I'm asking—"

"You will not ask this again," he warned her. "Just breathe, Mina. *Relax.*"

She sighed in exasperation and more than a little defeat, and then she continued to stand perfectly still. "Please, just move your fingers down…a little…*please.*"

He grasped her tighter and moved them higher. "No."

She trembled, but she didn't fight him.

"That's it, sweet Mina. Just breathe. And relax. And *listen.*"

Her chest rose and fell like a turbulent ocean tide, fluctuating with every breath.

"If Damian had chosen you, you would be dead right now." His voice was an icy rebuke. "Do you understand what I am saying? He is not a patient dragon. He is not a moral prince."

Her ears perked up as she tried to process his words. "Is he crueler than you?"

Dante laughed, and it was a haunting, wicked sound. "Damian would just as soon behead you as wed you. What he would have already done to you in this field would take months to recover from, if, indeed, you ever did."

Mina cringed. "And Drake?"

"Drake is not Damian. He is as noble as our kind can be, but he has no heart for war, no mind for elaborate strategy, no imagination for the schemes of our enemies. He cannot protect you from the threats within this realm, and there are many."

Mina shivered. "And you wish to *protect* me?" she scoffed.

"I wish to possess you—it is one and the same for a dragon."

Mina shook her head, still struggling to remain calm, to understand what he was trying to tell her: How could he possibly make a distinction between himself and his brothers? "You are all dragons."

"Yes," Dante agreed. "And that is why you must proceed with caution." When she didn't respond, he continued: "When you run, sweet Mina, the *dragon* gives chase. When you tell him *no*, he imposes *yes*. When you tell him he cannot have you, he *needs* to dominate you. He is not human. He does not think or reason. He is master of this realm, and if you tell him he is not, he will show you otherwise. Do you understand what I am saying?"

Mina suppressed a reservoir of mounting fears and tried to simply concentrate on Dante's words. It wasn't as if she had not heard them before, dozens of times, while being reared in the Keep: Dragons were predatory animals, beasts of instinct. They ruled with absolute power; resorted to force whenever they were defied; and exacted justice, swiftly and without mercy. They were powerful beyond measure, ruthless without restraint, and cunning without equal. She knew all of this, better than most. Still, she had not made the connection when it came to a dragon lord and his Sklavos Ahavi. Somehow, she had believed they would possess a gentler nature when it came to their females, their breed mates, their futures.

At least she had hoped...until now.

"So, when I question you, the beast responds?"

"He rises to the surface *quickly,* dear Mina."

"And when I tell him not to touch me—"

"He wishes only to force your submission."

She swallowed a lump in her throat. "And when I run…"

"He will *always* pursue you."

"And if I fight him?"

"He could hurt you."

"And you?"

"I am a dragon."

"Never a man?"

"I am *trying* to be a man as well as a prince." He spoke in a guttural snarl. "Only now. Only here. Only *for you*."

Mina finally understood.

And once she did, she recognized Dante's ferocity for what it was, an internal war between the prince and his beast. The hands that trembled, yet still remained *beneath* her breasts; the voice that rose and fell with dominance, reflecting tenuous control; the alpha creature that insisted upon her obedience—all were beholden to the dragon. "Forgive me, milord," she whispered.

"For what?" he said as his body stiffened.

"For my insolence and defiance. For displeasing you."

"Do not toy with me, Mina." His voice was laced with glacial warning.

Mina heard him clearly, the words beneath the words. "Is he close?" she asked, referring to his beast, not knowing if she really wanted the answer.

"So…*very*…close," he said softly.

Mina forced her hands to her side, ignoring the proximity of Dante's thumbs to her most intimate anatomy. She inhaled deeply and tried to concentrate on something—*anything*—that would bring her mind back to a peaceful state: the color of freshly bloomed tulips in the spring, the sound of the Draconem River as it swept through the *commonlands* valley; Raylea's laughter, and the joy her little sister had brought her, before she had been taken to the Keep.

Dante's muscles began to relax and his iron hold softened.

She leaned back into him, giving way to the submission he craved, and he breathed an audible sigh of relief.

When, at last, he let go, he spun her around to face him. "Kiss me, Mina." It was as much a need as a test. The dragon was still angry, still searching for control.

Mina stepped forward into his arms, rose up onto her toes, and pressed her lips lightly to his, following the swirl of his tongue as it gently swept the outline of her lips. He growled—that *had* been him earlier—and then he backed away. "You are mine, Mina." Despite his burgeoning self-control, he snarled.

"Yes," she whispered. "Your Sklavos Ahavi."

"And when the autumn leaves turn, and the king gives you to me, I *will* take you in every way."

She gulped. "Until then?" If her words had been any more hushed, they would have merely been thoughts.

"You will come at my command. You will do as I please. And you will accept my feeding as well as my touch."

Mina didn't reply, but she did hold his gaze.

At least that was something.

"And you will stay clear of Damian as much as possible," he added. "He also has the right to command you, so heed my warning, Mina. If you displease him, he will kill you before the Autumn Mating. And no one will punish him for the deed."

Mina nodded, understanding, as grave as the reality might be. "And Pralina? Is she also a threat?"

He tilted his head, considering her question. "She can be, but not like Damian."

Mina bit her bottom lip. "Anyone else?"

"Oh," Dante said, "*everyone* else: the warlocks in the east; the *shadows* in the west; the ancient Malo Clan of my father's enemies; the castle servants, when they are jealous or being petty; the Lycanians across the sea; and Wavani, the witch. You were protected at the Keep, and now you are here at Castle Dragon. You are on your own for the next five months."

Mina dropped her head in despair, even as she nodded with growing awareness. "And that is why you wished to show me fruit and flowers…and places to *hide*."

He looked off into the distance, and his silence said it all.

"Is there no one I can trust?"

"Oh, there are always servants you can trust, but their loyalty ebbs and flows; however, there is one who will always remain faithful: Thomas the Squire, a nine-year-old boy who has been with us since he was orphaned at age two. His allegiance is not *entirely* with my father."

Mina didn't dare ask what that meant. Surely, Dante Dragona was loyal to the king, without question or hesitation, but then why did he speak so cryptically about this squire? She curtsied as she had been taught in the Keep. "Thank you," she said, not knowing what else to say.

He took a measured step forward, but only halfway. "Come to me." He crooked his pointer and middle fingers in a microscopic gesture, much like he had done earlier.

Mina stepped slowly forward until her toes were touching his. She looked into his eyes and held his penetrating gaze.

He stared at her so intently, it was almost hypnotic. And then he ran his fingers through her hair, traced her jawline with his thumb, and trailed the back of his hand lightly along her throat, across her collarbone, and over her breasts, stopping to trace the outline of each areola.

She shivered and gasped, but she didn't protest. Her heart pounded in her chest, and she willed it to slow down.

"Don't ever forget what I am, Mina," he said in a chilling voice. And then, much like he had done with Pralina, he straightened, shrugged his regal shoulders, and inclined his head. He was all at once as calm, clear, and steady as a crystal pond.

He whistled for the horses, and the two magnificent beasts pranced eagerly to their lord's side. He gestured toward the white gelding and nodded, returning to his original intent. "Take your mount, Mina."

As before, his voice was a quiet command.

ABOUT THE AUTHOR

Tessa Dawn grew up in Colorado where she developed a deep affinity for the Rocky Mountains. After graduating with a degree in psychology, she worked for several years in criminal justice and mental health before returning to get her Master's Degree in Nonprofit Management.

Tessa began writing as a child and composed her first full-length novel at the age of eleven. By the time she graduated high-school, she had a banker's box full of short-stories and books. Since then, she has published works as diverse as poetry, greeting cards, workbooks for kids with autism, and academic curricula. The Blood Curse Series marks her long-desired return to her creative-writing roots and her first foray into the Dark Fantasy world of vampire fiction.

Tessa currently splits her time between the Colorado suburbs and mountains with her two children and "one very crazy cat." She hopes to one day move to the country where she can own horses and what she considers "the most beautiful creature ever created" -- a German Shepherd.

Writing is her bliss.

Printed in Great Britain
by Amazon